George Darley

Sylvia

Or, The May Queen, a Lyrical Drama

George Darley

Sylvia
Or, The May Queen, a Lyrical Drama

ISBN/EAN: 9783744787505

Printed in Europe, USA, Canada, Australia, Japan

Cover: Foto ©Andreas Hilbeck / pixelio.de

More available books at **www.hansebooks.com**

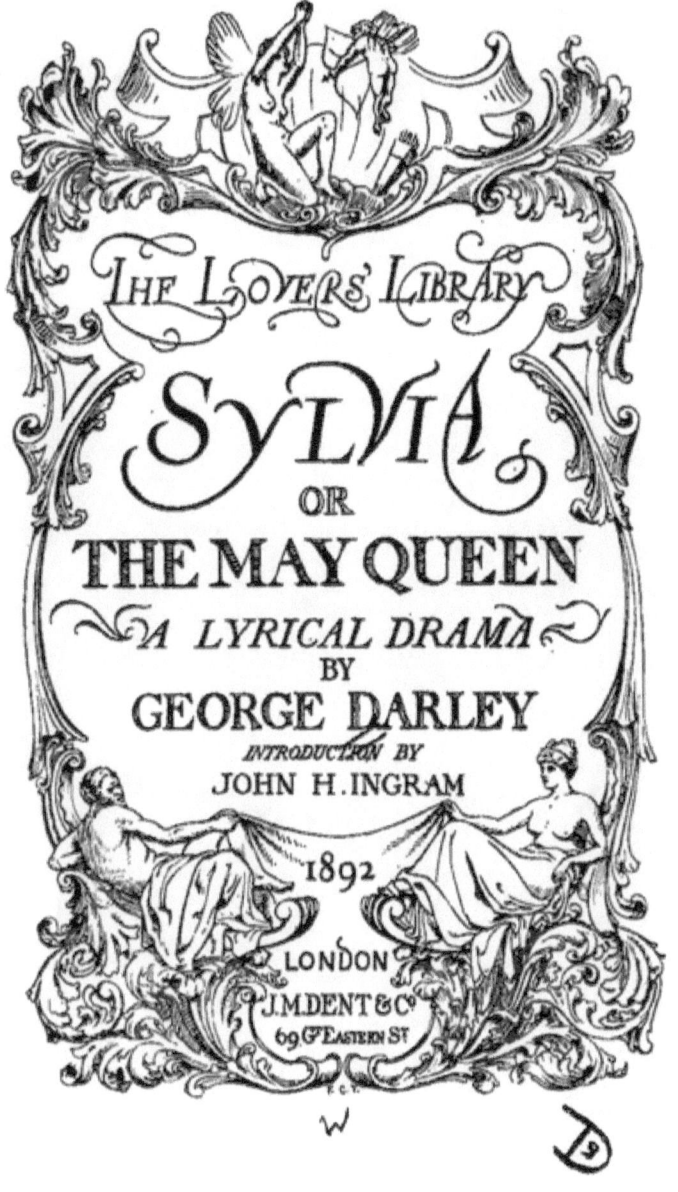

THE LOVERS' LIBRARY

SYLVIA
OR
THE MAY QUEEN
A LYRICAL DRAMA
BY
GEORGE DARLEY
INTRODUCTION BY
JOHN H. INGRAM

1892

LONDON
J. M. DENT & Co
69 Gt Eastern St

George Darley.

IN 1836, Miss Mitford, a leading spirit among the *literati* of her day, writes :— "I have just had a present of a most exquisite poem, which old Mr Carey (the translator of Dante and Pindar) thinks more highly of than any poem of the present day—'Sylvia, or the May Queen,' by George Darley. It is exquisite —something between the 'Faithful Shepherdess' and the 'Midsummer Night's Dream.'"

Half-a-century ago, George Darley, author of the poem thus alluded to, although now known only to a select few, was numbered among the poets of his people. He lived in an age of poets, and yet Carey, no mean judge, held his poetry highest. Lord Tennyson, whose own early lyrics were yet young, was so struck by Darley's power, that he volunteered to defray the cost of publishing his verse. Mrs Browning, another youthful poet, praised "Sylvia" as "a beautiful, tuneful pastoral," and her future husband, Robert Browning, was deeply impressed by it and its influence. We have his own authority for stating that it did much to determine the form of his own early dramas. That "Sylvia" charmed Coleridge, and many other lesser men of his generation, is only natural.

What is the "Sylvia" thus commended, and who its author, Darley? Miss Mitford, whilom the leading authority for all published about the poet, in her wonted good-natured, well-meaning repetition of unreliant gossip, condenses his story into these words:—"The author (of 'Sylvia') is the son of a rich alderman of Dublin, who disinherited him because he would write poetry; and now he supports himself by writing in the magazines."

As a matter of fact, the poet was not the son of Alderman Darley; he was not disinherited because he wrote poetry, and only the third assertion had a grain of truth in it. Such few biographical *data* as are known, and as are needed to be known, are as follows :—

The poet's father, Arthur, inherited a small independency from his father, George Darley, of the Scalp, County Wicklow. He married a cousin, who is remembered as "a woman of singular beauty and intelligence," and had several children, all of whom became more or less distinguished in their various ways.

George, the eldest, was born in Dublin, in 1795. His parents leaving their native land for the United States, the future poet, accompanied by two sisters, was left in charge of his paternal grandfather, with whom he remained until ten years of age. The boy had become a great favourite with the old Wicklow Squire, notwithstanding the fact that even at that time he was "much more full of thought than able of speech, being afflicted with a hesitation, which increased as years went on."

His parents returning to Dublin, George had to leave his Wicklow home, and give up his pleasant pony rides with his grandfather. He was placed in charge of a tutor, and, after the usual scholastic routine, was enabled to proceed to Trinity College, Dublin, where he did not graduate until 1820. The lateness of the age at which Darley took his degree was doubtless due to the want of confidence induced by the impediment in his speech, "his mask," as he not inaptly styled his affliction. This same wretched infirmity retarded his success, and embittered the whole of his future life. Some College honour or scholarship which he contended for, and from his intellectual superiority appeared certain of gaining, was snatched from his grasp at the vital moment, his physical trouble rendering him too nervous to succeed. Utterly disgusted, he forsook his native city, and did not visit it for years. Determined to devote himself to literature, Darley took up his abode in London, and there, in 1822, published his first volume of verse.

"The Errors of Ecstasie," this first volume, was somewhat incorrectly described as "a dramatic poem." It consists mainly of a dialogue between a Mystic and the Moon, and although not deficient in imagination, nor devoid of occasional beauties, neither it nor the "other pieces" which accompanied it, gave great promise.

Darley was not long in London before he made the acquaintance of many leading *literati*, but the impediment in his speech frequently deterred him from

mixing in congenial society.   Writing to a critic
whose friendship he was desirous of acquiring, he
says, "I would call, or ask you to call, but that
conversation with me is a painful effort, and to
others painful and profitless.   I am an involuntary
misanthrope, by reason of an impediment which
renders society and me burthensome to each other.
My works, whatever be their merit, are the better
part of me—the only one I can at all commend to
your notice."   Probably his extreme sensitiveness
caused him to exaggerate the extent of his infirmity,
although he described it as "a hideous mask upon
my mind, which not only disfigures but nearly
suffocates it," as he gradually became intimate with
so many of the choicest spirits of his age, not even
excluding the critic already referred to.   Canon
Livingston, indeed, states that "when completely
at ease in conversation with any congenial spirit, or
reading aloud, or declaiming from his favourite Eliza-
bethan authors, the defect in his speech disappeared."

That this defect did do much to sour Darley's
temper at times and preyed upon his mind cannot be
denied.   Procter says that he was "once tempted by
this physical ailment to travel as far as Edinburgh,
to consult a professor of elocution who professed to
cure similar defects.   The remedy, which appeared
to consist in causing his pupils or patients to utter
all their words in a sort of chant, produced no per-
manently good effect."

Darley's connection with some of the most pro-
minent London periodicals, and more particularly
with the *London Magazine*, naturally gave him
admission into the literary coteries of the metropolis.

He made the acquaintance of Lamb, Talfourd, Miss Mitford, Chorley, Sir Henry Taylor, Lords Tennyson and Houghton, Southey, "Barry Cornwall," and others, but his correspondence shows that his extreme sensibility to remarks other than laudatory on his own works must have rendered a long and familiar friendship with him very trying and uncertain. Miss Mitford may not be very exact in her assertion that Darley's disappointment at " not being acknowledged as one of the great poets of the age " caused him to acquire the "most intolerant fastidiousness and determination to disallow all merit in other writers —such as Scott and Wordsworth, for instance, and, indeed, every poet in every language—except Shakespeare and Milton," but his letters and critiques show not only his own sensitiveness to want of appreciation, but his difficulty to appreciate merit in others. Without any intentional unkindness, he was sarcastic ; and Procter, who long retained his friendship, admits that his stammer having thrown him out of society, the "loneliness produced melancholy, and sometimes a little acerbity in his humour; " and Canon Livingstone quotes the words of one who knew him well, to the effect that "his manner varied according to his mood and his companions. He was often somewhat of a Diogenes, silent and brooding, subject to fits of gloom and abstraction. At other times he would be vigorous and sarcastic. But, when he chose, he could be a delightful companion, for he was brimful of knowledge and steeped in poetry. His taste and feeling for music were exquisite."

It was under the pseudonym of "John Lacy " that

Darley's contributions, commencing in July 1823, first appeared in the *London Magazine.* He wrote a series of critical papers on the "Dramatists of the Day," chiefly with a view of showing to what a degraded state dramatic poetry had fallen. Amongst contemporary writers he singled out two for commendation, "a woman and a boy," as he remarked. Joanna Baillie, nowadays not appreciated at her worth, and Beddoes, were the dramatic poets whose works he selected as exceptions to the general mass of rubbish then doing duty for the drama. Darley's great but deserved praise of "The Bride's Tragedy" undoubtedly confirmed Beddoes in his devotion to the poetic drama, and inspired him to continue his labours in that direction.

In this series of papers on the drama, Darley made a noteworthy admission which should not be overlooked by his readers. Referring to the curious, out-of-the-way phrases and self-manufactured words which even in those days he habitually made use of, he remarks, "When I cannot find *one* authentic word to express a compound notion or principle, my horror of circumlocution obliges me to coin new and barbarous, but I hope not inappropriate terms." This custom, not without much to be said in its defence when moderately resorted to, ultimately became so habitual with our poet as to be a blemish and disfigurement of his later works.

Besides the letters referred to, Darley contributed various articles in prose and verse to the *London Magazine,* then the chief means of introducing many of the best living authors to the public. His best story, "Lilian of the Valley," appeared therein, and contained the immensely popular lyric of "I've been roaming." Well adapted to the voice, and displaying marked facilities of rhythm, the song deserved the popularity it acquired, yet acquired more perhaps by the reputation of the music it was wedded to by Horn, and its singing by Miss Paton, than by its own intrinsic merit. As a poem, it is surpassed by other far less known lines by Darley.

In 1826 our poet collected and published some of his tales under the title of "The Labours of Idleness; or, Seven Nights' Entertainments," as by "Guy Penseval." The prose and verse of this forgotten volume are alike graceful and charming.

In 1829 appeared "Sylvia," Darley's *chef d'œuvre*. It is difficult to characterise this work properly without appearing extravagant. As a poem and as a story it is equally charming. The plot is ingenious and the characters interesting, and as a play, well acted and adequately mounted, "Sylvia" should attain popularity. Here and there it is disfigured by the most curious naïveté, and, at intervals, lapses into such bathos, that the reader is inclined to think the poet is intentionally jesting with his judgment. Darley partly acknowledged these blemishes. Writing to Miss Mitford, he says :—

"You are quite right about 'Sylvia;' the grotesque parts offend grievously against good taste. I acknowledge the error, and deplore it. But the truth is, my mind was born among the rude old dramatists, and has imbibed some of their *ogre* milk, which gave more of its coarseness than strength to my efforts.   And, again, ' Sylvia ' was written in the gasping times of laborious scientific engagements. All its prose especially was what a boiling brain first threw up to the surface, mere scum, which I never intended to pass for cream."

Notwithstanding such drawbacks, trivial as compared with its manifold beauties, "Sylvia" is full of fascination.   It is replete with exquisite fantasy, poetry, pathos, and imagination.   The introductory portions to each act, although not always necessary for the story's development, are so metrically charming and artistically beautiful that no lover of verse would willingly part with them.   They mostly begin in a stately or subdued style, but, as the poet proceeds, his wild Celtic fancy breaks its curb and carries him into clouds of metaphor as marvellous as they are musical, although often the flight ends by a hasty and undignified descent to commonplace earth.

Thoroughly original as is the drama in its inception and treatment, reminiscences of Shakespeare's lighter moods frequently recur.   The hero and heroine were evidently suggested by Ferdinand and Miranda, and much of the faery action shows how deep had been the influence of " The Midsummer Night's Dream." Nephon is a near relative of Puck, and Morgana Titania's twin-sister, whilst Andrea is a loquacious and travelled Bottom.   Ararach and his friends, fashioned on the memory of Milton's Pandemonian imps, are, as was to be expected, far less interesting and less realisable than the pretty faery-folk, yet the description of the Fiend-king's hall and its *entourage* is not deficient of grandeur, nor, indeed, unfit to rank

with the hall of Eblis in "Vathek." Some of the lyrics
interspersed about the play are most daintily delicate,
and some—such as the lovely, musical serenade,
" Awake thee, my lady-love "—will linger long in the
memory. Darley's faery verse is among the loveliest
in the language ; at times is even sweeter than
Drayton's, and is as fantastic as Shakespeare's own.

The *dramatis personæ* in " Sylvia," unlike those in
Darley's other dramas, have distinct individualities,
which they generally manage to retain, although
towards the end of the play, it must be admitted,
the author seems somewhat to tire of his puppets,
and they grow more indistinct, whilst he lapses into
lengthy interludes of unnecessary descriptive verse.
Many of these descriptive passages, however, are
highly imaginative, and should be in themselves
accepted as proofs of their author's poetic powers.
" Sylvia " may be confidently trusted to preserve
Darley's name from oblivion.

The London Magazine did not exist many years, and
several members of its staff, including Charles Lamb,
" Barry Cornwall," and Thomas Hood, transferred
their services to the youthful *Athenæum.* Darley
also having apparently forsaken poetry, joined the
band of famous *literati*, who, by the aid of Mr Dilke,
were giving the leading literary journal its first start
on its career of success. After the publication of
"Sylvia," Darley forsook poetry, or appeared to do
so, for some years. He travelled abroad, supporting
himself mainly by his letters on Art.

Chorley, in his " Reminiscences," thus refers to
Darley's artistic contributions : " At the time when

my connection with the *Athenæum* began, this strange, reserved being, who conceived himself largely shut out from companionship with his brother poets by a terrible impediment of speech, was wandering in Italy, and sending home to the journal in question a series of letters on Art, written in a forced and affected style, but pregnant with research, unborrowed speculation, excellent touches by which the nature of a work and of its maker are characterised. The taste in composition, the general severity of the judgments pronounced, might be questioned; but no one could read them without being stirred to compare and to think. In particular, he laid stress on the elder painters, whose day had not yet come for England—on Giotto, on Perugino, on Francesco Francia, and on Lionardo da Vinci. To myself, as to a then untravelled man, the value of these letters was great indeed."

As Canon Livingstone points out, Darley was, indeed, one of the first to appreciate the early Italian painters. His letters on Art did much to prepare the thinking public for an appreciative reception of the tenets of the " Pre-Raphaelite " school. Whether his literary critiques in the *Athenæum* were so well regarded is scarcely a moot point. Chorley avers that, on his return to England, Darley took up the position of dramatic reviewer in the most truculent and uncompromising fashion, and treated some of the best favoured authors of the day with relentless severity. That something can be said, and well said, on the other side, the following words from the obituary of Darley in the *Athenæum* of the 28th

November 1846 show :—"As a critic, it would be difficult to rate him too highly. Though his manner might be too uncompromising, and his language made, perhaps, too poignant by characteristic allusions, distinctions, and similes, to suit those who shrink from the more severe aspect of truth—though his periods were at times 'freaked' with eccentricities of phrase which, in most other persons, would have been conceit—his fine and liberal organisation, which made him sensible to poetry, painting, and music, and to their connection—his exact and industriously gathered knowledge — above all, his resolution to uphold the loftiest standard and recommend the noblest aims, gave to his essays a vitality and an authority which will be long felt. Intolerant of pretension, disdainful of mercenary ambition, and indignant at sluggishness or conceit, he will be often referred to by the sincere and generous spirits of Literature and Art as one whose love of truth was equalled by his perfect preparation for every task that he undertook, and whose praise was worth having—not because it was rarely given, but because it was never withheld save upon good grounds."

Although it was not until 1839 that Darley printed any more poetry, save a few fugitive pieces in the periodicals, it is · probable that he never abandoned it entirely. The little success "Sylvia" gained, save among his own small circle of poets, discouraged him from publishing for a time. In the above year, he printed and circulated among his literary acquaintances a bizarre production entitled "Nepenthe." It is a startling manifestation of

Darley's facility of rhyme and musical rhythm. It contains passages of such glowing passion and glittering thought, such a bewildering exuberance of language, coupled with such complicated meta- phors and eccentric phraseology that one is disposed to agree with Miss Mitford, that "there is no reading the whole poem, for there is an intoxication about it that turns one's brains."

As a matter of fact, "Nepenthe" is a fragment, only two cantos of it having appeared in print. The opening verses are characteristic of the poet's better style :—

> " Over a bloomy land untrod
>   By heavier foot than bird or bee
> Lays on the grassy-bosomed sod,
>   I passed one day in reverie :
> High on his unpavilioned throne
> The heaven's hot tyrant sat alone,
> And like the fabled king of old,
> Was turning all he touched to gold."

Unfinished, disconnected, and incomprehensible as was "Nepenthe," its author was as anxious as ever about his readers' opinions. Some passages from a letter he wrote to Miss Mitford on the subject will equally well display Darley's epistolary powers, his egotism, and his intense sensitiveness to the critical opinions of others :—

"I cannot refrain, even at the risk of egotism, dear Miss Mitford, from expressing my pleasure and pride at your reception of my sorry little poetical tract 'Nepenthe.' Praise in general is to me more painful than censure, compliments as formal as those of ' the season ' from visitors, the frozen admiration of friends, I shudder in the heart at all this ; but one word of real enthusiasm, such as yours, is happiness, hope, and inspiration to me. Such as yours, I say, for when, together with being enthusiastic, praise is discriminative, it becomes to me what a feather is to an eaglet ; argue as we will, the spirit cannot soar without it. Mine has been, I confess, for a long time like one of Dante's sinners, floating and bickering about in the shape of a *fiery tongue*, on the Slough of Despond. If it ever has risen, 'twas an *ignis fatuus* for a moment only. Seven long years did I live on a charitable saying of Coleridge, that he sometimes liked to take up ' Sylvia.' What you say of her and ' Nepenthe ' will keep the pulse of hope (which is the life of the spirit) going, so that I shall not die inwardly before the death of the flesh. Many do, it is my firm belief, who, alas ! have had still more ambition, and less success than I. Murder is done every night upon genius by neglect and scorn. You may ask, could I not sustain myself on the strength of my own approbation ? . . .

"Believe me, I am far above the vulgar desire for *popularity*. I have none of that heartburn. Indeed, who of any pride but must feel as high as scorn above public praise when we see on what objects it is lavished ? Should I stand a hair-breadth more exalted in my own esteem by displacing for a day such or such a poetaster from his pedestal? But, candidly, judicious praise is grateful to me as frankincense, partly, no doubt, for the love of fame, born with us like our other appetites, and greatly do I feel from its being the proof that my supposed path towards the Centre of Light is not an aberration ? . . .

"Your preference for 'Nepenthe,' an unfinished sketch, to 'Sylvia,' a completed poem, gives me confidence in your judgment. It shews me you have, what is so difficult to meet with, a substantive, self-existent taste for *poetry itself*, when you can thus like storyless abstraction better than a tale of some (though little) human interest—not that the latter should be unappreciated where it occurs, but it *alone* is usually thought of. . . .

"The double mind seems wanting in me; certainly the double experience, for I have none of mankind. My whole life has been an abstraction, such must be my works. I am, perhaps, you know, labouring under a visitation much less poetic than that of Milton and Mæonides, but quite as effective, which has made me for life a separatist from society. . . .

"Were my knowledge of humanity less confused than it is, I apprehend myself to be still too much one-sided for the making a proper use of it. Do you not expect so from 'Nepenthe'? Does it not speak a heat of brain mentally Bacchic? I feel a necessity for intoxication (don't be shocked, I am a mere tea-drinker) to write with any enthusiasm and spirit. I must think intensely or not at all.

"My health is an indifferent one ; a tertian headache consumes more of my life than sleep does, and worse than this, not only wasting it, but wearing it down. And I have to scribble every second day for means to prolong this detestable headachy life, to criticate and review, committing *literary fratricide*, which is an iron that enters into my soul, and doing what disgusts me, not only with that day, but the remaining one. . . .

"Another hateful result of a solitary life, it makes me very selfish. Indeed, I doubt if it be not the mother of as many vices as idleness, instead of so much wisdom, and what not, it is said to hatch. Swift, you know, says, 'There are many wretches who retire to solitude only that they may be with the devil in private.' Man is surely a most gregarious animal; we ought all to put our minds together as near as the other beasts do their noses. I say this to shew you that my misantbropy is compelled, and that my mind has not *grown hairy* like that of many another anchorite, as well as his body."

In 1840, Darley published his "Thomas à Becket." It is the poorest of his dramatic works, although at the time of its appearance he evidently regarded it as his masterpiece and the corner-stone of his future fame. Writing to " Barry Cornwall," he characteristically says :—

"I am, indeed, suspicious, not of you, but of myself ; most sceptical about my right to be called ' poet,' and therefore it is I desire confirmation of it from others. Why have a score of years not established my title with the world ? Why did not ' Sylvia,' with all its faults, ten years since ? It ranked me among the *small* poets. I had as soon be ranked among the piping bullfinches.

" Poets are the greatest or most despicable of in-

tellectual creatures.   What with ill-health, indolence,
diffidence in my powers, and indifference (*now*) to
fame, I feel often tempted to go and plant cabbages,
instead of sowing laurel seeds that never come up.
Verily, I court the mob's applause, and care about
its censure as much as Coriolanus did; but unless
selected judgments are edified, where is the use of
writing for the All-seer's perusal and my own.

"Glad 'Becket' pleases you so far, but dissatisfied
(with myself, mind!) that it has only induced you to
skim it.   For Heaven's sake, unless it *force* you to
read it thoroughly, cram it into the blazes!   No
poetic work that does less is worth a fig-skin.

"Many persons, as well as you, dislike 'Dwerga;'
to me it seems, of course, the highest creation in the
work.   I wrote it with delight, ardour, and ease; how,
therefore, can it well be overwrought? which would
imply artifice and elaboration.   I *think* you'll like it
better some time hence.   T. Carlyle wrote me a
characteristic letter; compares 'Becket' to 'Götz von
Berlichingen!' and predicts vitality.   Miss Mitford
pronounces me Decker, Marlowe, and Heywood
rolled into one!   Others too are favourable, but see
what my great friend, the editor of the *Athenæum*,
has done for me."

Neither the author's own self-satisfaction, nor the
absurd applause of his friends, can obtain the vitality
predicted for "A Becket."   Owing to the highly
tragic nature of the story dealt with, the work is not
entirely devoid of dramatic interest, and might even
pass muster as a stage play; but of poetic talent it is
peculiarly deficient.   Nor are any of the *dramatis*

persona humanly interesting ; they are only lay figures which their creator is unable to vitalise. The reader cannot feel any solicitude for the fate of Fair Rosamond, or A Becket, or of King Henry, the chief personages of the play : the best, and, as Miss Mitford truly remarks, "The most original scene is one in which Richard is represented as a boy—a boy foreshowing the man, the playful, grand, and noble cub in which we see the future lion."

In the same year that "A Becket" was published, its author contributed to "Finden's Tableaux," then under Miss Mitford's editorship, a far less pretentious, but really more poetic, production. "The Harvest Home," although only written to illustrate an engraving is, in parts, a fairly good example of Darley's lyrical powers. The opening lines well display his idiosyncrasies :—

> " While on my knee within the myrtle shade
>   My silent lyre did stand,
> Upon my shoulder, like a feather laid,
>   I felt a little hand."

Although Darley again and again, in works published or left in manuscript, continually attempted to produce dramas, it must be confessed that he did not possess an aptitude for that branch of literature. His true vein was lyrical, and even "Sylvia" does not contradict, but rather confirms this opinion. It is a matter for real regret that some of his best work has never been published, and has probably perished. The posthumous volume of his "Poems," edited by R. & M. J. Livingstone,* contains several

* " A Memorial Volume for private circulation."

musical and beautiful lyrics, extracted from the manuscript of "The Sea Bride." This play, if we may judge from the specimens left of it, would have proved no unworthy companion to "Sylvia" itself. As an example of the sweetly musical verses with which it abounds may be fitly cited the following "Dirge," sung by Mermen :—

> " Prayer unsaid, and mass unsung,
>   Deadman's dirge must still be rung :
>   Dingle-dong, the dead-bells sound !
>   Mermen chant his dirge around !
>
> " Wash him bloodless, smooth him fair,
>   Stretch his limbs, and sleek his hair :
>   Dingle-dong, the death-bells go !
>   Mermen swing them to and fro !
>
> " In the wormless sands shall be
>   Feast for no foul gluttons be :
>   Dingle-dong, the dead-bells chime !
>   Mermen keep the tone and time !
>
> " We must with a tombstone brave
>   Shut the shark out from his grave :
>   Dingle-dong, the dead-bells toll !
>   Mermen dirgers ring his knoll !
>
> " Such a slab will we lay o'er him
>   All the dead shall rise before him !
>   Dingle-dong, the dead-bells boom !
>   Mermen lay him in his tomb !"

Several pieces in the same little book are autobiographical in character. They are replete with sorrowful regrets, expressions of frustrated ambition, and unsatisfied longings for poetic fame. Continually is the poet found sighing at the thought of his own unnoted grave, or vainly endeavouring to manifest contempt for the renown he never lived to acquire. This latter feeling is shewn in such pieces as "Memento Mori," an inscription for a tombstone, and the former more poetically in "The Lament." From these idiosyncratic verses may be quoted the following lines :—

> " Above my earth the flowers will blow,
>   As gay, or gayer still than now !
>   And o'er my turf as merrily
>   Will roam the sun-streaked giddy bee,
>   Nor wing in silence past my grave :
>   The bird that loves the morning rise,
>   Whose light soul lifts him to the skies,
>   Will beat the hollow heaven as loud,
>   While I lie moistening in my shroud
>   With all the cruel tears I have !

> " No friend, no mistress dear, will come
>   To strew a death-flower on my tomb ;
>   But robin's self, from off my breast,
>   Will pick the dry leaves for his nest
>   That careless winds had carried there :
>   All but the stream—compelled to mourn,
>   Aye since he left his parent urn—
>   Will sport and smile about my bed
>   As joyful as I were not dead—
>   Neglect more hard than death to bear !

> " Alive, I would be loved of *One*,
>   I would be wept when I am gone ;
>   Methinks a tear from Beauty's eye
>   Would make me even wish to die—
>   To know what I have never known !
>   But on this pallid cheek, a ray
>   Of kindred ne'er was cast away,

> And as I lived most broken-hearted
> So shall I die, all—all deserted,
>   Without one sigh—except my own!"

Less conventional in phraseology, and higher in tone, are the following lines styled "The Fallen Star," also to be found in this valuable and interesting posthumous volume :—

> "A star is gone! a star is gone!
>   There is a blank in Heaven,
> One of the cherub choir has done
>   His airy course this even.
>
> "He sat upon the orb of fire
>   That hung for ages there,
> And lent his music to the choir
>   That haunts the nightly air.
>
> "But when his thousand years are passed,
>   With a cherubic sigh
> He vanished with his car at last,
>   For even cherubs die.
>
> "Hear how his angel brothers mourn—
>   The minstrels of the spheres—
> Each chiming sadly in his turn
>   And dropping splendid tears.
>
> "The planetary sisters all
>   Join in the fatal song,
> And weep this hapless brother's fall
>   Who sang with them so long.
>
> "But deepest of the choral band
>   The Lunar Spirit sings,
> And with a bass-according hand
>   Sweeps all her sullen strings.
>
> "From the deep chambers of the dome
>   Where sleepless Uriel lies,
> His rude harmonic thunders come
>   Mingled with mighty sighs.

" The thousand car-borne cherubim,
    The wandering eleven,
All join to chant the dirge of him
    Who fell just now from Heaven."

In 1841 Darley again attempted to attract public
notice by another dramatic work. "Ethelstan, King
of Wessex," this new venture, was prefaced by some
characteristic remarks. "These hands," says Darley,
"would fain build up a cairn or rude national monument . . . to a few amongst the many heroes of our
race. . . . 'Ethelstan' is the second stone, 'Becket'
was the first, borne thither by me for this homely
pyramid. . . . The meditative pilgrim has stopped
to applaud my labour, the man of practice has
bestowed on it a cold approval, as a profitless,
romantic project, too much out of the present taste,
creditable to my dwarfish strength, but demanding
a giant's; while the busy world of wayfarers pass
it by unseen. 'Hope must be the portion of all
that resolve on great enterprises.'. . . I have, moreover, been in many cases consoled by the enthusiasm of strangers for the indifference of friends.
. . . Such opinions are indeed a 'portion' realised
beyond any promise of Hope, and all power of
Fortune : half the possible harvest is housed, which
should, so far as regards *self*, content an ungrasping
cultivator of his poetic field. A more comprehensive
and divine ambition would wish to see its efforts
generally beneficial, but of this half portion I fear to
be still disappointed ; it waits on genius as large as
the ambition."

"Ethelstan" was in some respects an advance on

"Becket," but as a drama is a failure. The characters have no vitality, and their conversations alternate between bombastic grandiloquence and ludicrous colloquilism.   There is a straining after, and frequent copying of archaic models, likely to repel the student of dramatic literature.   The imitations of Danish and Saxon ballads interspersed about the work, although imitations, are lyrically successful, and are not unworthy of their parentage.

Besides the works already referred to, and others known to have existed in manuscript, Darley edited, with a hastily written introduction, the works of Beaumont and Fletcher ; also wrote many literary and artistic critiques and some mathematical volumes.

During the five-and-twenty years Darley lived in England and abroad he saw but little of his family, and revisited his native country but rarely.   In November 1846, his health, as his correspondence shows, never strong, finally succumbed, and on the 23rd of the month he died in London, aged fifty-one, of decline.

One of his cousins, who knew him intimately, states that " his figure was tall and graceful ; his natural movements very striking as he walked ; his thoughts seemed to influence unconsciously every movement of his body.   His manner had much dignity, and conveyed at once that he was a man of commanding intellect.   His face was decidedly handsome, the features well cut, the forehead large, mouth very expressive.   The pale face bore a melancholy expression, and the intellect and imagination—both in constant exercise—left visible traces of their presence."

The best peroration of his life's short story is the Epitaph he wrote for himself :—

    " Mortal, pass on !—leave me my desolate home,—
      I ask of thee no sigh—I scorn thy tear !—
      To this small spot let no intruder come,—
        The winds and rains of Heaven alone shall mourn
          me here ! "

JOHN H. INGRAM.

Note.—Thanks are due, and are hereby gratefully tendered, to Miss Darley and Canon Livingstone (the poet's cousins) for various items of biographical interest, and for permission to use letters and poems herein quoted.   **J. H. I.**

Preface.

THE present Work is founded, in some measure, on a trifling story—"Lilian of the Vale," which the Author published not many years since. That story being interspersed with lyrical pieces, he was solicited to adapt it for the stage ; but considering its deficiency in human interest, he thought its success would be on that account, if on no other, more than usually uncertain. However, containing a few incidents of the dramatic kind, it suggested the idea of building upon them an Opera, which might not be unacceptable. Accordingly, one or two scenes of the following piece were written with that design ; but, disheartened by the almost universal failure of modern dramatists, by the prospect of suspense and servility which lay before him in his undertaking, as also by a mistrust of his own powers in this the most difficult walk of poetry, the Author gave up his resolution of writing for the stage. Passionately imbued with a love for theatrical composition, it then only remained for him to modify the scenes already sketched, and to continue his work on the plan of a *dramatic poem*, which he has attempted in the following pages.

By the above change of object, the Author likewise proposed to himself the benefit of a perfectly unrestricted design, so as to afford him the best chance of

succeeding, when his faculties, such as they are, had
no obstacles to contend with beyond their own imper-
fection.   On the same principle of writing at the
greatest possible mechanical advantage, he has,
throughout the whole course of his work, indulged
his vein, whatever it happened to be,—serious or
humorous, didactic or descriptive; he has written
verse or prose, song or dialogue; followed the heroic
or the lyric measure; been " everything by starts, and
nothing long," according to the impulse of the
moment.   Under all these favourable circumstances,
if he has not succeeded in producing entertainment,
he will regret it most unfeignedly for the reader's
sake, and scarcely less for his own.

Lay me down, lay me down by the stream,
Where the willow droops over the wave,
And the heavy-headed flowers do dream, —
There I'll make my last couch i'the grave

And the winds aloft choral shall keep,
With the robin that sings me my dirge,
Whilst the streamlet shall lull me to sleep
With the hum of its own little surge.

And the flowers above me shall grow,
Breathing softly to breathe not my rest,
And each sweet dewy morn as they blow
Drop a tear, bright and pure, on my breast

G D

Nov. 3 —

Facsimile of Darley's Hand-writing.

Characters.

ROMANZO.
ANDREA. *His Servant.*
GERONYMO.

SYLVIA.
AGATHA. *Her Mother.*
STEPHANIA.
ROSELLE. } *Peasant Girls.*
JACINTHA.
Peasants, &c.

SPIRITS.

MORGANA. *Queen of the Fairies.*
NEPHON.
OSME.
FLORETTA.
Fairies.

ARARACH. *King of the Fiends.*
GRUMIEL.
MOMIEL.
Demons.

The Scene lies in Italy, amongst the Apennines.

Sylvia;

or,

The May Queen.

ACT I.

Scene I.

 DEEP-DOWN valley, with a stream ;
Fit haunt for a poetic dream :
A cot fast by the water-edge,
A bower, and a rustic bridge ;
The grass as green as dewy Spring
Had just beswept it with his wing,
Or the moist splendour of the Morn,
Did every glistening blade adorn :
As soft the breeze, as hush the air,
As Beauty's self were sleeping there.
Enter ROMANZO on the heights,
Who sings the song our Author writes.

ROMANZO. O beauteous valley ! grassy-coated moun-
      tains !
Soft flowery banks, sweet pillows for unrest !

C

O silent glen of freshly-rolling fountains,
    If there be peace on Earth, 'tis in thy breast !
                                        [*Descends.*

At length, Romanzo, stay thy wandering feet :
Here be thy home, here be thy resting-place.
I've often heard the road to Paradise
Lay through the gates of Death ; it is not so—
This is Elysium, yet I have not died !
Or Death has come so softly, that I never
Heard even his footfall : he has taken me
When I was sleeping on some bank of roses,
And only said—Sleep on !   O beauteous scene !
Beyond what Hope, or fairy-footed Fancy,
Ever could lead me to !   The sunny hills,
Lightening their brows, appear to smile at me,
So lost in sweet astonishment.   Even I
Could smile, who have not smiled since I could feel.
The melancholy God loves me no more ;
My spirit bursts forth in song (Joy's eloquence),
And like yon tremulous nursling of the air,
Perch'd on and piping from a silver cloud,
I cannot choose but pour my strain of praise
To this most beautiful Glen.

  Beautiful Glen ! let the song of a Rover
Awake the sweet Echo that lies on thy hill ;
  Let her say what I say of thy beauty twice over,
And still as I praise let her mimic me still.   [*Echo.*

  Beautiful Glen of sweet groves and sweet bowers !
My voice is unworthy to praise thee alone :
  Let all thy sweet birds tell to all thy sweet flowers
The tale that I teach them in words of their own.
                                        [*Birds.*

Beautiful Glen of the white-flowing torrent !
If Spirit or Nymph be grown vocal again,
  Let her tune her sweet voice to the roll of thy
    current,
And mock me with murmuring—Beautiful Glen !
                    [*Voice within*—"Beautiful Glen !"

Ha ! what was that ?—was it a voice indeed,
Or but the repetition of my words
Made by some hollow cave ?—Never before
Came syllables from Echo's faltering tongue
So exquisitely clear !—Haply, I dream,
And this is all illusion : soft ! I'll prove it—
[*Sings*] "Beautiful Glen !"

            [*The voice repeats* "Beautiful Glen !"
Wondrous !—this is no voice
Of earth, yet speaks to mortal apprehension !
O who—who art thou, minstrel invisible ?
Tell me, who art thou that dost sing so sweetly ?

[*The voice sings*] Sing, and I shall answer meetly.

ROMANZO. Who art thou that sing'st so sweetly,
Echo, Echo, is it thou ?
[*Voice*] Now I'm asked the question meetly,
I will answer meetly now.
ROMANZO. Who art thou ?
[*Voice*] Perhaps what thou art !
ROMANZO. I'm a rover !
[*Voice*] So am I !
ROMANZO. Art thou mortal ?
[*Voice*] Not as thou art !
ROMANZO. Art thou spirit ?
[*Voice*] Come and try !
ROMANZO. Now I've asked the question meetly,
Answer me as meetly now.

[*Voice*] I have answer'd thee discreetly,
More I cannot answer now.

ROMANZO. Shall I believe in this?—Ears, can I
trust your evidence ? I have likened ye oft to those
wild sea-shells which are full of most delicate music
born in their own hollows : was this but the fan-
tastical creation of yours ? No ! it was plain as light;
and if unreal, then is yon marble dome but a vapour
of the imagination !—What meant this syren of the
air ? Why did it court me on ?—No matter ! As the
poor swimmer dives for a jewel at the bottom of the
perilous gulf, so must thou too, Romanzo, seek thy
fortune in the depths of this mystery ; though, like
him, the waves of ruin may o'erwhelm thee.—Ha !
what a palace is here ! a rural one !—Nature, thou
hast a Doric hand, but a most Corinthian fancy !—
Or is this, too, a work of enchantment ? Has it been
transported hither while I was dreaming, by some
genii, the mighty slaves of a magician, or raised by
the wand of fairy Maimoun, as we read of in the
tales of the East ?—To be sure, this jessamine tapestry
is thick enough to hide a less modest dwelling. How
prettily it smiles through the leaves ! like a russet
maiden holding a rose before her beauty to enhance
by concealing it. Does a woodman live here, or an
anchorite ?—It is the very retreat for an uncanonized
saint, or the snow-bearded tenant of a wilderness.
At home, father ?   [*Knocks.*

Enter AGATHA.

AGATHA.   Your will, signior ?
ROMANZO.   Pardon, good dame ! I have need of
that for my rudeness, ere I can expect any other
favour.   Pardon, I beseech you, for my intrusion.

AGATHA. It needs none, signior ! The traveller is welcome to my poor cottage, though but few enter it.

ROMANZO. Strange ! for I think its beauty might allure the steps of a courtier. Do many people inhabit this valley?

AGATHA. Two only, signior ; myself and daughter.

ROMANZO. Oh ! then it was she I heard just now sing so divinely ?

AGATHA. My daughter, signior ? no ; she is now far away on the hills, gathering wild flowers or simples.

ROMANZO. What then, do you keep a mocking bird ?

AGATHA. The echo, signior, is loud in this place : you are now standing on the plat we call *"Echo's ground."* Say *echo !* and it will be thrice answered.

ROMANZO. Ay, but can your echo maintain a conversation ?—for here was one, I assure you.

AGATHA. Nay, signior, I cannot account for it ; your senses must have been deceived.

ROMANZO. Perhaps so. [*Aside.*] But it is a mystery I will rather die than leave unravelled. [*Aloud.*] Prithee, dame, if a wanderer may presume on your good nature, will you afford me a night's lodging in your pretty bird-cage ?

AGATHA. Willingly, signior, if its poor accommodations may content you.

ROMANZO. Poor !—while the vine forms the gable of your tenement, and hangs at your window, you have meat, drink, and shelter together. Thanks, gentle hostess !

AGATHA. Pray walk in.

[*Exeunt into the cottage.*

Scene II.

A view like one of Fairy-land,
As gay, as gorgeous, and as grand :
Millions of bright star-lustres hung
The glittering leaves and boughs among ;
High-battled, domy palaces,
Seen crystal through the glimmering trees,
With spires and glancing minarets,
Just darting from their icy seats :
Pavilions, diamond-storied towers,
Dull'd by the aromatic bowers ;
Transparent peaks and pinnacles,
Like streams shot upward from their wells,
Or cave-dropt, Parian icicles.
  Green haunts, and deep enquiring lanes,
Wind through the trunks their grassy trains ;
Millions of chaplets curl unweft
From boughs, beseeching to be reft,
To prune the clustering of their groves,
And wreathe the brows that Beauty loves.
Millions of blossoms, fruits, and gems,
Bend with rich weight the massy stems ;
Millions of restless dizzy things,
With ruby tufts, and rainbow wings,
Speckle the eye-refreshing shades,
Burn through the air, or swim the glades :
As if the tremulous leaves were tongues,
Millions of voices, sounds, and songs,
Breathe from the aching trees that sigh,
Near sick of their own melody.
  Raised by a magic breath whene'er
The pow'rs of Fairy-land are here,
And by a word as potent blown

To sightless air, when they are gone,
This scene of beauty now displays
Both flank and front in sheets of blaze :
Spirits in an ascending quire
Touch with soft palm the golden wire :
While some on wing, some on the ground,
In mazy circles whirl around :
Kissing and smiling, as they pass,
Like sweet winds o'er the summer grass :
NEPHON and OSME chief are seen,
In heavenly blue, and earthly green,
The one and other : both unite
With trim FLORETTA veiled in white ;
And mincing measures small and neat,
Mimic the music with their feet.
After their dance is done, the chorus
Hints something new descends before us.

CHORUS OF SPIRITS.

Gently !—gently !—down !—down !
   From the starry courts on high,
Gently step adown, down
   The ladder of the sky.

Sunbeam steps are strong enough
   For such airy feet !—
Spirits, blow your trumpets rough,
   So as they be sweet !

Breathe them loud, the Queen descending,
   Yet a lowly welcome breathe,
Like so many flowerets bending
   Zephyr's breezy foot beneath !

MORGANA *descends amid sweet and solemn music.*

MORGANA.   No more, my Spirits !—I have come
        from whence
Peace, with white sceptre wafting to and fro,
Smoothes the wide bosom of the Elysian world.
Would 'twere as calm on Earth ! But there are some
Who mar the sweet intent.   Ev'n in these bounds,
Ararach, wizard vile ! who sold himself
To Eblis, for a brief sway o'er the fiends,
Would set up his dark canopy, and make
Our half o' the vale, by force or fraud, his own.
We must take care he do not.—Where's that ouphe ?
That feather-footed, light-heeled, little Mercury ?
That fairy-messenger ? whom we saw now
Horsed on a dragon-fly wing round the fields ?
Come out, sir !—Where is Nephon ?

NEPHON.   Here am I ! here am I !
        Softer than a lover's sigh,
        Swifter than the moonbeam, I
        Dance beefor thee duteously.

MORGANA.   Light gentleman, say whither hast
thou been ?
NEPHON.   Over the dales and mossy meadows
green.
MORGANA.   Doing the deed I told thee ?
NEPHON.   Else would I fear thou'st scold me !
MORGANA.   Led'st thou the Rover downward to
the glen ?

NEPHON.   Down, down to the glen,
        Through forest and fen ;
        O'er rock, and o'er rill,
        I flattered him still ;
        With chirp, and with song,
        To lure him along ;

Like a bird hopping onward from bramble to briar,
I led the young Wanderer nigher and nigher !

MORGANA.   None of your idle songs ! speak to me
plain.
NEPHON.   I laid a knotted riband in his path,
Which he took up ; kiss'd—'twas so fine !—and put it
Into his breast : *Ting ! ting !* said I, from out
A bush half down the dale : he gazed.   *Ting ! ting !*
Said I again.   On came he, wondering wide,
And stumbling oft, ha ! ha !—but ne'er the less,
He followed sweet *ting ! ting !* down the hill-side,
E'en to the bottom : where I mock'd and left him.
MORGANA.   I'll bring thee a sweet cup of dew
for this,
Cold from the moon.
NEPHON.   Meantime, I'll drain a flower
Fill'd with bright tears from young Aurora's eye.
MORGANA.   Skip not away, sir !—List what thou
must do.
False Ararach doth love the gentle maid
Who shepherds in this vale : nay, he would have her
Sit on his iron throne, and rule with him.
She has oft wept, and call'd Heaven pitiless,
So that I've laugh'd to see her needless pain.
She is my favourite, and I will protect her :
I've search'd the wilderness of Earth all o'er
To find her a fit bridegroom : this is he
Whom thou hast guided hither.
NEPHON.   A trim youth !
MORGANA. Be it thy business to search out the wiles,
Prevent the malice, curb the violence,
With which the spiteful monarch will assail him.
Ev'n now he scents some new-come virtue here,

And plots its quick destruction.   Swift, away !
Thou'lt see me nich'd within a hovering cloud,
Pointing thee what to do.   When thou would'st know
How to direct thyself, look up to Heaven,
And light will fall upon thee.   Swift, away !
      NEPHON.   Away ! away ! away !
            Away will I skip it !
            Away will I trip it !
   Flowers, take care of your heads as I go !
           Who has a bright bonnet
           I'll surely step on it,
  And leave a light print of my mannikin toe !
        Away ! away ! away !   [*Vanishes.*
  MORGANA.   I've seen a man made out of elder pith
More steady than that puppet !—Yet, he's careful,
Even where he seems most toyish.—Virgin Spirit !—
Come hither, fair Floretta !

  FLORETTA. As the murmuring bird-bee comes,
        Circling with his joyous hums,
        Red-lipt rose, or lily sweet—
        Thus play I about thy feet !

  MORGANA. Thou art the. Queen of Flowers, and
      lov'st to tend
Thy beauteous subjects.   Thou dost spread thy wing
Between the driving rain-drop and the rose,
Shelt'ring it at thy cost.   I've seen thee stand
Drowning amid the fields to save a daisy,
And with warm kisses keep its sweet life in.
The shrinking violet thou dost cheer ; and raise
The cowslip's drooping head : and once didst cherish
In thy fond breast a snowdrop, dead with cold,
E'en till thy cheek grew paler than its own.

FLORETTA. Ay, but it never smiled again ! Ah,
   me !

MORGANA. Go now, since beauty is so much thy
   care,
Sweetness and innocence—go now, I say,
And guard the human lily of this vale.
Follow thy mad-cap brother, and restrain
His ardour with thy gentleness.

FLORETTA. Ere thou say *Begone !* I'm gone :
   'Tis more slowly said than done !

                         [*Vanishes.*

MORGANA. Osme, thou fragrant spirit ! where art
   thou ?

OSME. Rocking upon a restless marigold,
And in its saffron, leafy feathers roll'd ;
But with a bound I'm with you here—behold !

MORGANA. Hast thou been sipping what the wild
   bee hides
Deep in his waxen cave, thou smell'st so sweet ?

OSME. No : I would never rob the minstrel-thing,
That lulls me oft to sleep with murmuring,
And, as I slumber, fans me with his wing.

MORGANA. My gentle elve ! — Come thou, come
   thou with me :
I've an apt business for thy strength.   Sit here,
On my light car, and be the charioteer ;
Guide thou my trembling birds of Paradise,
That prune themselves from this dull earth to rise,
And cry with painful joy to float amid the skies.
Ascend ye other Spirits all with me !

CHORUS.

See the radiant quire ascending,
   Leaving misty Earth below,

With their varied colours blending
  Hues to shame the water-bow.
Slowly, slowly, still ascending
  Many an upward airy mile !
To the realms of glory wending,
  Fare thee well, dim Earth, awhile !

Scene III.

The jasmined cottage in the glen
Presents its flowery front again :
Opening its gem-bestudded door
Is seen the Youth we saw before ;
He finds his Hostess on the green,
Who at her purring wheel hath been,
Since Phosphor raised his ocean-cry,
As nimbly be sprang up the sky,
His towering walk to 'gin betimes,
Lest Titan catch him as he climbs.
    Were I an artist I could etch
E'en now a pretty moral sketch :
The widow, with a serious look,
Conning her distaff as a book ;
Her eyes on eartbly duties bent,
Her mind on bigher tbings intent :
The youngster worships all be sees
As he were well content with these :
His the broad brow of admiration,
Hers the pale smile of resignation ;
His Grief is old, his Joy is new,
Her Joy is dead,—and Sorrow too !
Now, while they talk, in silence I
May underneath the rose tree lie.

ROMANZO. It is true! it is true!—This scene is too bright for an illusion!—Joy! ecstacy! I tread the earth! I hear the song of birds, and the fall of waters!—No! my senses could not so far deceive me! —Oh, how I feared, on waking, to find all that had passed a dream!—Sun, I thank thee, for dispelling with thy glorious light the mists of doubt and apprehension!—Nay, here is living testimony!—Good morrow, hostess!—Why, Fortune herself does not turn the wheel faster!

AGATHA. I wish she were obliged to turn it as steadily.

ROMANZO. Would that she had your beechen wheel, and you her golden one, even for a single round!

AGATHA. She would be a fool to make the exchange; and I, perhaps, no better.—May she be as kind to you, signior, as you wish her!

ROMANZO. Thanks, my good dame!—What! are your birds always so merry at matins? or is it me whom they welcome so joyfully?

AGATHA. You and the sun, I suppose, signior.

ROMANZO. Ah! I doubt whether the god has not the greater share of the compliment.—But, hostess! kind hostess, what angel voice was that I heard this morning? It thrilled my very heart-strings with pleasure!

AGATHA. Are you quite sure it was an angel you heard, signior?

ROMANZO. Truly, I would think it!

AGATHA. Else, I should have said it was no more divine a being than my daughter.

ROMANZO. Oh, for the love you bear her, say not so!—If she be such a cherub, Earth cannot pretend

to keep her !—Yet, by our Lady, we have need of a
saint or two here, for there is no lack of sinners.

AGATHA.   Oh, sir, you must not talk so wildly.
My daughter rises when the lark is but shaking the
dew off his breast ; she is almost as light to mount
the hills as he the heavens ; and it is nearly as hard
to get the one as the other to speak without singing.

ROMANZO.   Whither has she gone ?

AGATHA.   Do you see that little bird I spoke of,
hitching himself, as it were, up the sky ?

ROMANZO.   Yes, as if he were scaling an invisible
ladder.   What of him ?

AGATHA.   You might as well climb the stepless
air and catch that voice, that singing speck in the
clouds—for he is now no more,—as overtake my
Sylvia.   But they will both, wild ones as they are,
sink at once into their nests when their duty calls them.

ROMANZO.   Well, I must be patient.—From your
speech, good lady, I surmise—pardon me—that you
have not always lived in this secluded valley.

AGATHA.   Not always, sir, as you say.   My for-
tunes were once higher, though my wishes never.   Had
my husband been but left to me, I had not regretted
the loss of worldly treasures.   He, however, died, in
the field of glory, as they call it,—and that was also
the death of my happiness.   In that fatal plain of Aost—

ROMANZO.   Ha ! it is something to have fallen
with Bayard !

AGATHA.   Little to the widow :—Hark !—

[*Song without*]   Oh, sweet to rove
                      The wilds we love,
Soft glade, smooth valley, and mountain steep—

AGATHA.   She comes !   My bird—

ROMANZO. The voice! the lovely voice!—Show thyself, chantress! lest I go mad with expectation!

AGATHA. Pray, signior, retire into the arbour: hide yourself in the foliage. Silent is the nightingale when the stranger's eye is upon her.—Ah! roamer!

[SYLVIA *appears on the bridge.*]

AGATHA. Come hither, truant! and let age play the child in thy bosom.—Where hast thou been, wanderer! tell me?

SYLVIA. Oh, sweet to rove
    The wilds we love,
Soft glade, smooth valley, and mountain steep;
    Ere birds begin
    Their morning din.
Bright sun abed, and bright flowers asleep.

AGATHA. Come to my arms!

ROMANZO (*within the arbour*). Is it a sylph or wood-nymph that glitters before me?

SYLVIA (*approaching*).
    While Cynthia looks
    Still in the brooks
And sees her beauty begin to wane:
    Down in the dell
    Her silver shell
Seems hung from Heav'n by a sightless chain.

    To see the elves
    Prepare themselves
To climb the beams of the slanting moon,
    Or swiftly glide
    In bells to hide
And press their pillows of scent at noon.

> To pluck the gems
> That bow the stems
> Of flowers, in meadow or secret glen ;
> To ope their breasts,
> And trim their crests,
> And spread their beautiful looks again.

AGATHA.   No longer ! no longer !—

SYLVIA.   Oh, sweet ! oh, sweet !
> And sweeter yet,
> My crown of roses, my pearls of dew,
> To come ! to come !
> Once more to home,
> With flow'rs, and kisses as sweet, for you !

ROMANZO (*Bursting from the arbour*).   Angels are brighter than I dreamt them !

SYLVIA.   Ah ! Morgana defend me !

AGATHA.   Fear not, my daughter.   Thou knowest there is no evil spirit can enter this half of the glen. Look not so strange at him.

SYLVIA.   Evil !—Oh, if that creature be evil, I can not be good !—It is not one of Morgana's courtiers, is it ?   They take all shapes that are delightful.

AGATHA.   This is my daughter, sir ; daughter, this is our guest.   [*Aside.*]   Youth salutes youth as rose doth rose—they blush at each other, and sigh— I must be prudent here ; these new acquaintances will be near ones, though they keep the matter so silent.

SYLVIA.   Some bee hath got into my bosom ; out, stranger !

ROMANZO.   Lady ?

AGATHA.   I will bestir me now: you shall taste our fruits and cream.   [*Lays a table.*]   Grapes here

—bread there—honey—Both! both through the heart !—Two birds upon one bough with the same arrow !—Cupid is a rare sportsman !—So ; ay—A leaf to garnish these strawberries—Love at first sight is an old adage, but I never thought till now it was a true one.—I must know more of this stranger.

ROMANZO.	O fairest !
SYLVIA.	O rarest !
Both.	Creature of no mortal birth !
ROMANZO.	If thou'rt woman,
SYLVIA.	If thou'rt human,
Both.	Heaven is sure outdone on earth !

ROMANZO.   Pearly brow and golden hair,
Lips that seem to scent the air,
Eyes as bright, and sweet, and blue,
As violets fill'd with orbs of dew.
O fairest !

SYLVIA.   O rarest ! &c.

SYLVIA.   God-like form, and gracious mien,
As he once a king had been !
Glory's star is on his brow,
He is King of Shepherds now !
O rarest !

ROMANZO.   O fairest ! &c.

AGATHA. Come ! come !—you are playing the birds' parts, and they will play yours at this fruit-table, if you thus leave it them.—Come !

> [*They sit down to table.*
> *Scene closes.*

Scene IV.

A shadowy dell, from whence arise
Fen-pamper'd clouds that blot the skies,

D

And from their sooty bosoms pour
A blue and pestilential shower.
High in the midst a crag-built dome
Ruder than Cyclops' mountain-home,
Or that the blood-born giants piled
When Earth was with their steps defiled.
Lightning has scorch'd and blasted all
Within this dark cavernous hall ;
Through every cranny screams a blast
As it would cleave the rocks at last ;
Loud-rapping hail spins where it strikes,
And rain runs off the roof in dykes ;
And crackling flame, and feathery sleet,
Hiss in dire contest as they meet ;
Tempests are heard to yell around,
And inward thunders lift the ground.

In front a dismal tomb-like throne,
Which Horror scarce would sit upon :
Yet on this throne doth sit a thing
In apish state, misnamed a king ;
A ghastlier Death, a skeleton,
Not of a man, but a baboon.
His robe a pall, his crown a skull
With teeth for gems, and grinning full ;
His rod of power in his hand
A serpent writhing round a wand :
With this he tames the gnashing fiends,
Soul-purchased to assist his ends ;
Yet still they spit, and mouthe, and pierce,
If not with fangs, with eyes as fierce,
Each other—while behind they seek
Their sly revenge and hate to wreak.

Hear now the WIZARD (with a grin
Meant for a smile) his speech begin.

ARARACH.   Silence, cursed demons!—Listen to
        me, or
I'll strike ye dumb as logs!—Breathe no more flames
In one another's faces, but pen up
Each one his fiery utterance while I speak!—
Silence, I say!—and cower before me, slaves!—
I must and will have all this Valley mine!—
    Demons. You must and shall!
    ARARACH. Silence, and down!—hear me!—
We've sworn indeed—but what are oaths to us?
Oaths are to bind, where there's some touch of honour,
Though not enough. It were a crime against
The majesty of Sin, for us to keep
An oath; and honour is dishonourable
Amongst the fiends, whose glory is in shame,
We'll break the truce, I say!
    Demons. We will! we'll break it!
    ARARACH. Silence!—'Tis true, I and that witch
        Morgana
Have battled long about this place: we halved it
At our last contest, when her ivory spear
Wounded my basilisk, and made him bite me
Here in the wrist, or I had crush'd the minion.
    Demons. Vengeance!—war!—war!—
    ARARACH. Down with that trump!—not so!—
We must be cunning, for yon queen is wise.
I'll first secure the mountain-girl I love;
Sylvia, the shepherdess: who else may fly,
Scared by the din of arms: perhaps be scorch'd
Or kill'd amid the fray.—Spirits and Horrors!
    All. Ay! ay! ay!
    ARARACH. Which of you loves a mischievous
        adventure?
    All. I, my lord!—I!—I!—I!

ARARACH.   That will hurt men,
Please me, and gain great praise?—Who speaks?
All.   All! all!
ARARACH.   But there's some danger in it: you
    must face
Morgana and her imps.   What! does that fright ye?
Cowards;—Will none leap forward?
                     [GRUMIEL *comes forward.*
Ha! brave Grumiel!
  MOMIEL.   (*Coming forward*)
Master, I'll do the mischief; let me, pray thee!
Were it to kill a baby in its play,
Ravin a leaguer'd city's corn, or drain
The travellers only well i' the sanded wilds,
That his dry heart shall crumble; yea, the beauty
Laid warmly in her bridegroom's treasuring arms,
Shall turn a corpse-cheek to his morning kisses
If thou wilt have it so.—Let me, I pray thee!
  ARARACH.   Good! Good!—Go both of ye!—
    Thou my bold slave!
And thou, my sly one!—aid him with thy strength,
And he will prompt thy dulness.
  GRUMIEL.   Hang him, poltroon!
Must I divide my glory with a knave
Who winks at a drawn blade?—a foul-mouthed cur,
That bites the heel and runs!
  MOMIEL.   Master, yon fool
Hath no more brains than a cauliflower; pray
Let him not go with me!—An alehouse board
Sets him to spell: he cannot count his fingers
Without a table book.
  GRUMIEL.   Curse ye, vile babbler!—hound!—
Mouse-hearted wretch!—
  MOMIEL.   How wittily he calls names,

Like an ostler's paraquito !

ARARACH.   Ye will prate,
Both of ye in my presence, will ye?—Take thou
    that—
And thou another? [*Strikes them*]   Ay, stand there
    and writhe,
But whine not, ev'n for pain.   Ye'll say, forsooth,
What ye would have!—Listen to my commands,
And do them to the tittle, ye were best!—
Go forth, but stealthily : we'll try at first
What may be done by craft.   I'd rather gain
One treacherous point, than win a battle-field.
Go forth, I say ; and use all smooth deceit
To wile the Maid into our bounds : or, if
She is too coy, and fearful, being warned
Of our intents by some sly ouphe, then hear
What ye shall do.   A youth has lately wander'd
Into this bourne, whom by my art I know
The witch hath for this Nymph selected spouse.
Him shall ye seize ; for he is all unversed
In these wild paths, and is a hot-brain, too,
That loves a deed of peril for its name.
If we could grip him, the elf-queen would scarce
Make up the loss : at least her present aim
Would be thus baffled, and our road left clear.
Ye know your business : off! and do it wisely!
Grumiel, be thou the master ; and thou, sirrah!
Counsel him to thy best.

MOMIEL.   [*Aside*]   Oh ay, I'll lead him!—
I'll be his Jack with the Lantern !

GRUMIEL.   Follow me,
Thou muttering slave !

ARARACH.   If you do take the youth,

Brain him not : do you hear me ?—We will keep
      him
Alive in torture here : perchance the Nymph
(Whom they will give love-potions) may be tempted
Thus to approach our realm, and lose herself
Ere she find him.   That were a triumph worth
Laying ten plots for.   Vanish !

    Demons.   Way for the King !

                        [*They vanish separately.*

ACT II.

Scene I.

T HE homestead of a thrifty peasant,
Quiet, secure, well-built, and pleasant ;
Its eaves are moist and green with age,
Its windows wattled like a cage :
From out the tell-tale chimney curl
Blue wreaths of smoke with easy whirl ;
A huge domestic elder tree
Shades the dear cot maternally ;
While the sweet woodbine on its walls
Sits weaving her fine coronals,
Dropping betimes a careless gem
From some loose twisted diadem,
And looking down as she would stoop
To pick her fallen jewels up.
In front a narrow garden blows,
With formal flowers set out in rows,
With gravell'd walks, smooth as the sands
Laid down by Triton's webbed hands ;
Neater, I ween, though not much ampler,
Than wee miss works upon her sampler,
And looking like a cit's parterre
Amid the mountain grandeur there ;

For some bred in the wilderness,
By contrast love wild Nature less
Than those who gasp within the town
To range the hill, and roam the down,
Loving wild loveliness alone
  The cottage-back, if you must hear,
Shuts out a liquid murmurer,
(But you may catch his sullen roar
More loud when opes the thorough-door,
And see him far a-field betray
With shining scales his serpent way.)
Ev'n in that Isle by Vesper fann'd,
Which all the world calls " Snug-man's Land,"
The land of heartfelt, homely bliss,
There's not a snugger cot than this.
One side leans oldly 'gainst the hill,
And t'other props a crony mill
That aye keeps clacking, clacking still ;
As if it never would have done
Its tale to its companion.
  Two smiling lasses (fair ROSELLE,
And STEPHANIA, a village belle)
Are seated at an oaken table
That scarce to bear the weight is able
Of fruits, and roots, and cates, and pies :
A flagon of portentous size
Stands, like the urn of ancient Po,
From whence his sea-bound surges go
Bellying, the table-foot beside ;
From which a wrinkle-smoothing tide
Pours the burnt traveller you see
Into his cup right frequently.
It is a quaint and humorous wight ;
His eye proclaims him : ANDREA hight,

More of his character I could
Discover, *certes*, if I would :
But pray let your own eyes and ears
Serve as your own interpreters.

ANDREA.   O my unfortunate Master ! O my kind
—O !—

STEPHANIA.   Another bowl of cream !

ANDREA.   Thanks, gentle signorina !—if it were
deep enough to drown me, miserable that I am ! it
would be only the more deeply welcome !—O sweet
and excellent [*drinks*] master !

ROSELLE.   Look what a tempting bunch of grapes !
Do pluck one.

ANDREA.   Are they good for a hoarseness ?

ROSELLE.   Better than a box of lozenges, I warrant them.

ANDREA.   Say you so ?—Then I will consent to
devour a sprig or two, for I am hoarse with lamenta-
tion and bawling.—O comely youth ! O taper young
gentlemen ! O kind, noble, chaste, sweet-spoken
vagabond master !—shall I ever behold—

STEPHANIA.   Such a cheese as the moon was
never made of ! I pressed it with my own two hands.
'Tis the purest, finest goat's-milk cheese — pray,
signior, have a slice of it.

ANDREA.   It will strengthen me for whooping and
calling, else I would not touch it for diamonds ! It
will make me *ma-a* like a he-goat on a rock-top when
he misses the beard of his charmer.

ROSELLE.   Indeed now, you must try our apricots
and walnuts. Here is another loaf hot from the
oven.

STEPHANIA. Do not spare the pasty; its fellow is in the larder. Help yourself to another cup of wine : the flagon is beside you.

ANDREA. Alas—I cannot.

STEPHANIA. Pray be entreated.

ANDREA. I am inexorable !—No ! I will abstain —mortify—I will make a desperate vow—Hear me, thou adorable flagon ! If ever I drink a single cup of thy contents, while my dear master—

ROSELLE. Nay, it is too late : you have had some half-dozen already.

ANDREA. The very reason I can take no more !

STEPHANIA. Wherefore, dear signior ?

ANDREA. Simply because there is no more to take ! the wine has evacuated its tenement ; the flagon is empty.

STEPHANIA. Run, dear sister ! Go : fetch out our mother's flasket of cordial. You can guess where it lies. It is better than a hogshead of ordinary wine. --Here it is.

ROSELLE. [*Filling out a goblet.*] Now, bachelor !

ANDREA. [*Taking the goblet.*] Do you see this vessel ? Do you mark its capacity and dimensions ? Well :—I have rained the full of this from either flood-gate, three-score of times at a modest computation, since I lost my unfortunate master yesterday morning. Can you wonder if my lachrymatories be in want of a replenishment ? [*Drinks.*]

STEPHANIA. Alas ! true-hearted youth !

ROSELLE. Forlorn creature !

ANDREA. I have drunk nothing but salt water from the brine-pits of mine eyes since my master mislaid himself among these villainous mountains. And that, you know, were sufficient to make me as

dry as a turnspit in the dog-days ; or the cook of a
ship's company on pickled allowance, in the latitude
of the line, at noontide, when the sun looks like a
red-hot shot in a furnace, and the air would stew
salamanders.

STEPHANIA *and* ROSELLE. True ! true !

ANDREA. I have spouted as much water through
my head as the lion on an aqueduct, or a whale in a
fit of sneezing. Verily, I never wept so much for
any two of my grandmothers, though the last left me
heir to all she had in the world, *videlicet:* her
blessing. Have you no sad verses to suit the occasion? no miserable rhymes? no ballad about love
and murder, or elegy on the death of a favourite lap-
dog? Pray consult your albums.

> [*Sings*] Oh, Sorrow was ever a thirsty soul,
> As Margery did discover ;
> For every tear she drank a bowl,
> That her eyes might still run over !
> [*Drinks.*

The melancholics always give me the poetics :
therefore, O sweet hostesses ! pity my hapless situation.

STEPHANIA. In what respect besides being a
melancholy poet ?

ANDREA. Oh, I have lost the most amiable,
provoking, excellent, incorrigible whistle-cap of a
master that ever poor fellow had since the days of
knight-errantry. The guide of my youth ! the
protector of my innocence ! the defender of my
virtue !—Here do I find myself like a distressed
damosel, or the Wandering Jew, in the midst of this
frightful wilderness, without knowing either how I

came into it, or how I am to get out of it : looking
as strange and bepuzzled as a flying-fish caught in the
shrouds, or a wild-man-of-the-woods in a show-box.
I have not even a word to put forth in excuse if a
shepherd's cur chose to ask me my business.   Wherefore and therefore :—O unfortunate Andrea ! O luckless Pimpinella ! O miserable Ribobolo ! O unfortunate, luckless, and miserable Andrea della
Pimpinella di Ribobolo !

ROSELLE.   What shall we do with him ? he is
again in a fit of the boetics.

STEPHANIA.   Pritbee, friend Andrea della Pimpinella di Ribobolo, do not frighten the squirrels.

ANDREA.   I must give vent to my passion ; I
must relieve my oppressed heart with an effusion of
some sort or other.   [*Drinks.*]

STEPHANIA.   Only that the cup has a bottom, you
might think it was a spy-glass.

ROSELLE.   He is going to balance it on his nose ;
stay a little.

ANDREA.   Would this bottle were pewter that I
might squeeze it !—Slidikins ! where did that other
sun come from ? No ! 'tis the sun and moon shining
together : excellent !—I find this wine begin to ele-
vate me.

[*Andrea in his chair is slowly raised from the
ground.*]

You need not draw away the table, though.—Why,
hostesses !—where are you going ?—Sinking !—sinking !—Mercy upon me ! do they live in a well ?

STEPHANIA *and* ROSELLE.   O strange !

ANDREA.   Have I been singing with Mermaidens?
—Down ! down !—still—Hew ! by Saint George and
the Dragon, they are on a mining expedition !—Out

upon ye, speculators !—Alas !—O !—Uds my life ! is
their father a pump-sinker ?

STEPHANIA.   Wonderful ! wonderful !

ROSELLE.   Hush, sister ! I have heard of these
moon-calves.   He is one, I am sure, by his roaring.

STEPHANIA.   And his great mouth.   Whither is
he going ?

ROSELLE.   Only to catch larks for his supper.   Or
may be his dam bleats for him : did you not hear
him cry out *the moon ! the moon !* this moment ?

ANDREA.   Now could I weep pitcherfuls !

STEPHANIA.   I thought he was a flighty sort of a
gentleman.   But lo ! where he rises !—Take care of
your hat, sir !

ROSELLE.   Hold on by a tree-top !

ANDREA.   Hold on by a fiddlestick !—Catch you
some root or tuft, or brushwood ! Get astride of some
bough, I tell ye ! O sinful pair ! what have ye been
doing that the fiend should carry you down in this
manner?

STEPHANIA *and* ROSELLE.   O friend Andrea,
what can you have done that you should deserve to
go to Heaven in such a hurry ?

ANDREA.   Take to your marrow bones ;—Kneel
—pray—confess,—out with all your iniquities !—
weep, children ! roar ! sing !—Have you no *pater*,
or *ave*, or *credo ?*—What do the fools gape at ?—
Begin !—Beat your breasts ! maul your petticoats !
take down the pride of your tuckers !—O miserable
women !—Tear your hands ! wring your hair !—Will
ye not ?—Did you ever see such a couple of uncon-
verted Magdalens ?

STEPHANIA *and* ROSELLE.   Alas ! alas ! he is
growing as small as a tom-tit !

ANDREA.   Son of my father ! they look like two
white mice at the door of a trap !—Farewell, hostesses !—good-bye !—O sad ! O marvellous !—they
are not the size of their noses !—Phew ! I begin to
smell brimstone and pitchforks.

STEPHANIA *and* ROSELLE.   Let us pray for his
safety.

ANDREA.   They are at it ! they are at it !—Now
is there some hope of their perdition from utter
salvation ! Obstinate jades ! they would not do so
when I told them.   Louder ! louder !—I can scarcely
catch a mumble.   Who the vengeance, d'ye think, is
to hear you at this height ?—They are sighing in
anguish and contrition.   Poor souls !—deeper and
deeper !—He has them now by the ankles : O kind
Satan ! send them a gentle swinging, if thou hast any
compassion in thy sooty bosom !

STEPHANIA.   Poor Andrea.

ROSELLE.   Poor signior Di Gobble-o !

Scene II.

Oh, have you known, fond youth, as I
What 'tis to climb the mountains high,
With a bright form of beauty o'er you,
Lighting the airy path before you ?
To see how wastefully the wind
Sweeps round and o'er, yet still unkind,
Nought but the fine small ankle shows
For all it flutters, flaps, and blows ;
Clasping indeed the slender knee
As smooth as chisell'd drapery,
And with its plastic breath pretending

To shape a Phidian beauty bending
Against it strength—yet leaving you
As wise as if it never blew ;
For still the envious kirtle dances
Just in the high-road of your glances !
   Something like this sweet agony
Haps to my hero, I can see ;
The sylvan girl before him glides
Like Oread up the mountain-sides ;
No finer form on Attic shore
Bold-eyed Apelles scann'd of yore,
Nor peeping gods, when Jove's free daughter
Lavish'd her white limbs on the water
With its loved burden proudly swelling,
While Dorian caves for joy were kneeling,
Triumphant tales of beauty telling.
But our young goddess doth exceed
This reveller on the ocean-bed ;
For, of a loveliness as rare,
She is as pure as she is fair :
Her snowy mountain-garb reveals
The charms alone no garb conceals,
Which, spite of that ensphering shroud,
Burst forth like moonbeams through a cloud.
   Silent, the rapt idolater
Of this fair wood-nymph follows her ;
Yet distant, too, which e'er it be
Revering her divinity,
Or that, perdue, his gleaming eye
May some neglectful beauty spy ;
Yet still to doubt and wonder given
At so much beauty under Heaven.
   She turns, and speaks !—Around her mouth
Breaks a slow smile : as when the South

Opens thy lips, O ruby rose !
And thy look brightens as it blows.

SYLVIA.   I am too light of foot, I fear, for you.
ROMANZO.   Are you of earth ? I see the bended
     grass
Fillip you off its shoulders like the dew
At glistening up-suntide.   You press the herb
As tenderly as mist.   Sure you have coursed
With Naiads after pearls on the quick stream,
That you can fleet so deftly : or bas Zephyr
Lent you his winged slippers ?
   SYLVIA.   O no ! no !
My sole companions until now have been
The wild bird and gazelle : haunting with them
Has made me near as buoyant.   Pardon me !
Sooth I forgot myself with our sweet talk,
And when I should be courteous, and restrain
My wonted pace, the music that I hear
Makes me dance onward like the thistledown
Timing its gait to the wind's eloquence.
But you are all to blame !
   ROMANZO.   Oh, I could follow you
To the world's bound ! o'er unsupporting seas
And snows infirm as light ! Methinks I could
Fleet across bottomless gulfs on the thick air,
And scale the cliffs that nought but sunbeams climb,
Borne up by aspirations towards your beauty.
I have oft dream'd
Of gliding by long leaps o'er the green ground
In breathless ecstacy : through plushy lanes,
Tree-sided ; and down sloping esplanades

Battening in sunlight ; along valleys dim,
High-terraced rivers, and wild meadow-lands,
Bending my easy way : by will alone,
And inward heaving, rais'd, I seem to flee,
With pleasant dread of touching the near grass
That brushes at my feet.   But this fine dream
Is now as dull as life ! Yon angel sun
Swims up the welkin not with half the joy,
The silent joy in smoothness, that I feel
Soaring up this hill-side so green with you:
   SYLVIA.   Why do I feel such pain to hear you
      speak ?
Your gentle voice thrills in my happy bosom
Like waters trembling in their fountain-cell
At hearing the groved nightingale.   Speak on.
   ROMANZO.   Dear Sylvia—
   SYLVIA.   I did never think my name
So beautiful before !   Have other men
Voices as soft as yours?
   ROMANZO.   The mountain air
Sweetens its tone.
   SYLVIA.   O no ! it was the same
Down in the vale, when you told in mine ear
Things that I understood not, though I wish'd.
Wilt say them o'er again ?
   ROMANZO.   Not now ; I dare not !
When you look back upon me with that brow
So golden ; all with curled sunbeams hung ;
Brightening above me into that sweet smile
Angelical,—I almost think you come
From Heaven to lead me thither.   That light garb
Floating behind you seems to part in wings,
And your ethereal form glides up the steep
As smooth and noiseless as it rose indeed

Spontaneous to its own cherubic sphere.
I could even kneel to thee !
   SYLVIA. Nay, sit you down
Upon this mossy bank o'er-violeted,
And we will gaze upon the vales below :
And we will spend an hour of rapturous talk—
And gaze—and talk—and read each other's eyes,
Blissful as birds : or pluck wild flowers and sing
To the hoarse-cadent waterfalls : or hymn
A lovely story out, and stop and listen
While the wind bears to echo the faint tale,
That woos its sweet way back to us again.
   ROMANZO. Oh, I am wrapt in glory !—Seem we
      not
Like two young spirits stole from Heaven to view
This green creation ; who with looks of praise
Sit murmuring on the early mountain-tops
In close ambrosial converse ?—Oh, look round !
Pleasure lies floating o'er the scenes beneath
Dissolved in the warm air ; and gorgeous Noon
O'er the ripe fields her yellow veil doth spread
So thick, mine eyes scarce pierce it.
   SYLVIA. Turn them here
And drink fresh wonder. Yon's my favourite haunt :
A winding elm-walk, by a silver stream
Ambling free-footed down the mountain's side,
Weetless of whither : till it falls at last,
With gentle wail that it must sleep so soon,
Over the rocky shelve into the lake,
The glassy-bosom'd lake, so deep and clear.
   ROMANZO. Methinks the boughs that keep it dark
      and cool,
Hang o'er the jetty marge in a fond dream :
Even their whispering speaks of sleepiness.

SYLVIA.   Look on the feeding swan beneath the
willows.
How pure her white neck gleams against their green
As she sits nesting on the waters !
    ROMANZO.   Beautiful !
She is the lady of the reed-girt Isles !
See ! how she swells her navigable wings
And coasts her sedgy empire keenly round !
She looks a bird of snow dropt from the clouds
To queen it o'er the minnows !
    SYLVIA.   Doth she not ?
Side-looking, slow, disdainful one !
    ROMANZO.   The bright,
The pearly creature!—Lone and calm she rides,
Like Dian on the wave when night is clear,
And the sleek west-wind smooths the billows down
Into forgetfulness, that she may see
How fast her silver gondola can boom
Sheer on the level deep.
    SYLVIA.   Behold yon rock
Down which a torrent shines afar : the noise
Is loud, yet we can't hear it.
    ROMANZO.   Partial heavens !
Oh, what a splendid deluge thou pour'st down
From out thy glorious flood-gates, on this vale !
Thickets, and knolls, slopes, lawns, and bosomy dells,
Scarce show their green for gold.   Yet, it is strange !
There is a melancholy in sun-bright fields
Deeper to me than gloom ; I am ne'er so sad
As when I sit among bright scenes alone.
    SYLVIA.   Perchance your fortunes are not of that
            hue,
And then it seems to mock them.—Come, your eyes
Are full of meditation's tears.   Come on !

I have a garland still to bind for you :
Come ! to the myrtle grove.

    ROMANZO. The myrtle grove !

    SYLVIA.   I'll teach you too how it behoves you
      walk
This valley.   Come !

    ROMANZO.   Sweet ! to the myrtle grove !

                              [*Exeunt.*

Scene III.

Down the bourn-side and up the dale
Observe a dim line across the Vale,
By sad and sun-green grasses made
A boundary of light and shade :
This is the running landmark drawn
Athwart the deep prospective lawn,
Sharing the Valley's length between
The Fiend-King and the Fairy-Queen.

Enter GRUMIEL *and* MOMIEL.

    MOMIEL.   Proceed, master !—proceed, thou in-
      fallible *vade mecum !*

    GRUMIEL.   Goad me not, fleering pest ! with thy
      long nails,
Else I will tear the skin from off thy back,
In straps ; or gouge thine eyes out.

    MOMIEL.   But, my lord,
We shall not catch our prey else—

    GRUMIEL.   Fogs on him !
And him that sent us ! and thee too, thou zany !
Come on, and thou shalt see there is no means
To pass without our limbo.

MOMIEL.   So ! his rush
Is out, I think !
   GRUMIEL.   Feel here ; a sightless plane
Of glass stands like a crystal wall, as high
As bridgy Heav'n : 'tis thinner than blown soap,
Yet strong as adamant to smoky natures
Like thine and mine : this is the jealous pale
And limit of our realm.   We cannot pierce it
Without a spell, and that would rouse Morgana.
Come hither ; strive to punch thy finger through,
Or break thy foot against it.
   MOMIEL.   No, my lord,
I'll use a tougher mallet—give me leave—
   GRUMIEL.   What wouldst thou do ?
   MOMIEL.   Why, take thee leg and arm,
And bounce thee 'gainst it like a battering-ram,
Till skull or wall should crack : better if both.
   GRUMIEL.   Thou that canst grin so like a wolf,
      howl too !   [*Strikes him.*
   MOMIEL.   I'll get thee plagued for this : I'll be
      revenged !
   GRUMIEL.   We must slouch home.
   MOMIEL.   Ay, and be scorch'd to fritters !
That is your wisdom !—No ; hear my device :
Let us creep serpent-wise along the ground,
Close by the wall, and trap the younker ranging.
   GRUMIEL.   Poh ! thou'rt a counsellor indeed ?
         How trap him ?
How should we lure him o'er ? first tell me that.
   MOMIEL.   I have a stratagem.   The heat is fierce.
And he will rage with thirst.   Do thou stand here,
With a deep bowl of Lethe in thy fist,
A little from the wall : thou hast a face,
A good bronze face, and Ethiop limbs to boot,

So may'st assume the statue.   If he thrust
A nostril through the wall, the deadly fume
Will cloud his brain, and through all lets he'll come,
Like a blind horse, to drink.   Stand till he tries
To bathe his lip in the fresh cup thou hold'st,
And then we'll seize upon him.

GRUMIEL.   Good ! I see it.
Vanish thou when he comes.   I will stand fast
As the unquarried rock ; and so present him
This maple bowl, crown'd with such juicy weeds,
And dropping such pure blobs, that he will drink
Though angels bid him hold.

MOMIEL.   Lie close ! lie close !   [*Exeunt.*
            Enter NEPHON *behind.*

NEPHON.   Ho ! ho ! I thought that I should catch
      ye ;
Snakes i' the grass, I'll over-match ye.
Here comes an instrument that shall
Work our advantage and your bale.
Hist ! hist ! Floretta !

            Enter FLORETTA.

FLORETTA.   Ay !—like you
    I have been eavesdropping too.
        Now I must like wind away
            To my virgin care,
        And entice her if I may,
            From this demon snare.
        Eve shall hang the clouds with scarlet
        Ere I rest me !   [*Vanishes.*

NEPHON.   Here's the varlet !—
      In the skylark's simple bed,
      Nephon, hide thy artful head.

            Enter ANDREA.

ANDREA.   I have heard of Pacolet and his horse,

that could fly from Constantinople to Rome by the
turning of a peg in his neck, and without the turning
of a hair on his body : for indeed he had none ; being
made, I think, of good dry oak, if it were not rather
Spanish mahogany.   But, for the most part, I have
always set down such matters as nothing better than
moral tales; with no more truth in them than is to
be found at the bottom of a well ; and of use only to
give youth a relish for history and learning.   Now
do I see the vanity of this age in pretending to cry
down such things.   What I have not I been soaring?
have not I been taking down a few cobwebs from
the "hazy canopy," as we say in rhyme? have not I
cut "the starry firmament" hither, on a four-legged
stool?   How many minutes is it since I was cheek by
cheek with a couple of frolicsome damsels, or rather a
still more kiss-provoking double tankard?—and now
—O sorrowful change !—I am only beside myself, in
this hideously beautiful valley?   O Master ! Master !
would I might see the fringe of thy skirt, or pick up
one of thy stray belts !—it would do to hang myself,
if I had no other consolation !

> [*An embroidered suit falls in different places
> about him.*]

So-ho, there !—Does it snow by the yard here ? and
in summer too?—Cloaks ! doublets ! indescribables !
—What ! are the clouds woollen-manufactories ! Is
Heaven any place for a tailor? could he soar thither
on his goose?—O fine !—If the fig-trees in this place
grow leaves equal to these, I have found out the site
of Adam's paradise.   They shall not long be in want
of a wearer.   'S life I they fit me like a new skin.
Now if I should meet Signor Romanzo I No matter ;
I would not bend a hair from my altitude : I shall be

as good a gentleman as he in my fourth generation.
O grand !—Now could I lead a troop of horse ?—O
magnificent Andrea !—Wert thou ever a plebeian ?—
But, alas ! of what use is all this splendour when
there is no one but myself to admire it ?

NEPHON.   Signior Andrea !

ANDREA.   Ahoy !—who squeaks ?

NEPHON.   Signior Andrea della Pimpinella !

ANDREA.   Santa Maria ! am I pinching the tail
of a grass-mouse ?—Where did it get my name,
though ?

NEPHON.   Signior Andrea della Pimpinella di
Ribobolo !

ANDREA.   Andrea della Pimpinella di Ribobolo !—
he has learnt it all as pat as my godfather !—only that
he sings it a little through his nose.   Where is this
mighty small-spoken gentleman ?—Hilloa, Signior
Nobody ! at what point of the compass must I look,
to be mannerly ?

NEPHON.   Consult your shoe-buckles.

ANDREA.   O pupil of mine eyes ! what do I behold ?—Art thou Gorgoglio, the son of the giant
Gorhellione ? or only a simple Patagonian from the
South Pole ?   What heathen ogress gave such an
enormity birth ?   Did Nature cut thee out of a
mountain ?—What art thou ?

NEPHON.   Look at my mustaches !

ANDREA.   Ay, I might have known thee for an
hussar by the ferocity of thy voice, and the stoutness
of thy figure : thou art all over tags and bobs too,
like an itinerant haberdasher.   What is thy name ?—
Grimbalduno, or Hurlothrumbo ?

NEPHON.   I shall not be loth to declare it upon
any gentlemanly occasion.

ANDREA. Lud-a-mercy! I did not mean to send your reverence a challenge! The very wind of your weapon would make flitches of me: slice me from nape to hip, like two moieties of a pig hung up i' the shambles. No! no! I have more wit than to have my skull laid open like a boiled rabbit's, or to die the divisible death of a walnut!

NEPHON. Will you walk then,—I mean, saunter?

ANDREA. So as your reverence has no blood-thirsty intentions: I am no dare-devil to encounter such a Goliath. But take care lest my foot happen to light on your reverence; it might squeeze your reverence into the capacity of a dollar: and by'r lady! I cannot undertake to distinguish your reverence while dame Earth keeps her beard unshorn. If I should step into a two-inch tuft, it's odds but I commit man-slaughter. Could not your reverence manage to take my heel by the elbow? We might then trot on brotherly together.

NEPHON. Take care of thyself, Master Andrea: there are man-traps hereabout. Leave me to my own discretion.

ANDREA. Agreed, your reverence: only re-member that if I shall chance, in raising my foot, to kick your worship to Grand Cairo, I shall not be bound to measure swords with you reverence for the insult.

NEPHON. Agreed! agreed!   [*Exeunt.*
Scene changes to another part of the woodland.

Enter ROMANZO AND SYLVIA.

SYLVIA. No farther, dear companion!—where yon stream
Tink'es amid the bushes down the vale,

The ground becomes unholy.

ROMANZO.   O sweet Sylvia !
I long to be thy champion, thy true Knight !—
Thy conquering smile upon me, with this sword
I'll undertake to blaze destruction
Through every demon cave——

SYLVIA.   Not for the world !
Thou must not be so venturous !

ROMANZO.   I would do
Some deed of high devotion, as of old,
Renowned Youths did for their lady-loves.
Prithee, assent !—with Heaven's good aid and thine,
Yon half o' the vale, now sable-green, and drear,
Shall bloom beneath thy fearless step like this ;
And thou shalt range it, as the palmy hind
Her forest walks unscared.

SYLVIA.   Do it, and make me
Fall from my happy state !—Wilt have me weep ?

ROMANZO.   Nay, kill me with a frown—if thou
        canst frown,
Ah ! strive not !—on thy candid brow a star
Shines cloudlessly, and oh, more constant bright
Than e'en the marble tutoress of a cave
Holds 'tween her heavy eyelids, when the moon
Has stolen upon her beauty.   'Tis in vain !
Thy lips are grave—no more !   Come, thou must
        smile !

SYLVIA.   Then do not pain my heart by talking
        thus
Of wild attempts : I'm satisfied with thee,
And do not wish thee greater ; nor a space
More wide for our sweet rambles.   Let me show thee
Carefully all the fatal bounds, that when

Thou walk'st, perchance, alone, thou may'st avoid
    them.
Then will we to the bower.

Enter FLORETTA.

ROMANZO.   What is here?
Sylvia !—see ! see !
  SYLVIA.   Peace ! 'tis a fairy !
One of the petty angels of this realm ;
We must be courteous to the gentle thing,
Or 'twill not hum its song.   Listen ! Oh, listen !
  ROMANZO.   Oh, Heavens ! I almost weep and
    laugh at once
To hear its silver words ; and see it tipping
Every fair-crested daughter of the field
With puny hand.—What ! doth it steal their leaves?
  SYLVIA.   Sweet friend, keep silence !

FLORETTA.   I do love the meadow-beauties,
      And perform them tender duties,
      So the fair ones let me use 'em
      For my brow, and for my bosom.
        Follow ! follow ! follow me !
        And I'll choose a brooch for thee !

      Here be pansies just a-blowing ;
      Here be lords and ladies glowing ;
      What a crowd of maiden blushes
      Court a kiss on yonder bushes !
        Follow ! follow ! follow me !
        And I'll get a kiss for thee !

      Down the slopy hillocks, sweetest
      Grows the blue pervinké, meetest

For a garland ; should the wreather
Cowslip choose, she may have either !
  Follow ! follow ! follow me !
  And I'll show them both to thee !

[*Exit, followed by* ROMANZO *and* SYLVIA.

Enter GRUMIEL *and* MOMIEL.

GRUMIEL.   Pugh ! I smell villanous mortality !—
Our prey is near.

MOMIEL.   Is this he striding towards us in seven-
leagued shoes, with a whole peacock's tail in his
bonnet ?

GRUMIEL.   Ay ; doth he not strut most wrathfully,
like a lobster-nosed alderman, or a new-made lord o'
the bed-chamber ?   A's a gallant fellow ! It must
be he !

MOMIEL.   Doubtless it must : he comes of a coach-
keeping family, at least ; for the smirk of my lady's
footman shines out in his visage : I warrant you now,
simple as he walks there, he can trace his pedigree
to Adam !

GRUMIEL.   Ay, and to popes and emperors ; he is
scarlet even to the tip of his nostrils.   Tell me that I
have not the eyes of discovery again, sirrah !

MOMIEL.   Faith, yes, to detect the pulp of a melon
under the coat of a pumpkin.   Are the seven wise
souls of Greece clubbed in thy politic person ?—
[*Aside.*]   There is nothing of the Narcissus about this
swaggerer ; a bulrush bred out o' the mire : he hath not
the look of a flower-gentle.   Some ass in the hide of
a zebra : some highwayman, that hath changed cloaks
with a cardinal.   But 'twill do ! this sot of a spaniel
here will get lugged for his mistake ; setting a scare-
crow instead of a woodcock.   I'll humour it !

GRUMIEL. Slink off, thou gibbering ape !—
I'll stiffen into metal, with the cup.

MOMIEL. Ay, thou'lt brazen it out, never fear
thee, like a saint upon a vintner's sign-post.—Here
he comes, walking as wide and crop-swollen as a
magpie in red spatterdashes.—How naturally that
brother of mine looks through glass eyes at nothing ?

Enter ANDREA ; NEPHON *behind.*

ANDREA. Paugh ! the sun, I think, is very in-
decorously hot ; nothing above lukewarm is fashion-
able : therefore Apollo is less of a gentleman than his
brother Phœbe, as we classically desecrate the night's
bright lunatic. 'Slidikins ! I melt like a waxen
image in the bodice of a fat landlady.—Oh, for
another pull at "our mother's flasket of cordial ! "
—What hoa ! Signior Grasshopper !—Could'st thou
pilot me to some well or stream? I'll set thee on the
back of a minnow for it, if thou lik'st such a cock-
horse.—The *homunculus* had almost slipped out of
my remembrance during the last minute. 'Slife !
'tis vanished out of my sight also !—Oh lamentable !
Ox that I am, I have trodden his little frogship into
a mummy ! his blood is upon my toe !—This comes
of walking with greatness ; this comes of conversing
with those that are above thee ; thou wilt be crushed
as a grain of wheat by a millstone ! Phial of Saint
Januarius ! what have we here? A noddling man-
darin-cup-bearer ! a Hottentot Granny-maid !—if it
be not rather a newly-cast chandelier walked abroad
from the foundery ! Is it the bottom of a brewer's
vat he stretches forth so courteously?—Oh, now I
have it ! 'tis a charity cup for the wayfarer, posted
here by some benevolent monks in the neighbourhood. I'll be bound for it though, the hospitable

gentlemen have not squeezed the best o' their vintage into it. Nothing, as I live! more precious than water, and that none of the most fragrant. Waugh! I hope the spring was not poisoned; nevertheless my tongue is drier than a camel's hoof, and I must soak it a little, if 'twere only to prevent it growing cloven. So, *Monsieur* Dumb-waiter, by your leave—

GRUMIEL [*seizing him*]. Dog! I have thee!

MOMIEL. Collar him! collar him! with thy brassy talons!

ANDREA. I am betrayed, like an innocent!—O thou treacherous mite! O thou iniquitous atom! O thou vile thumb of a man! would that I never—

MOMIEL. Chuck him under the chin for his brave speech-speaking : grip him fast by his thump-cushion arms, lest he overdo the action.

GRUMIEL. Drag him along, the field-preacher!

MOMIEL. Ay, to court with him! he shall preach before his majesty.

ANDREA. Beseech ye, noble Abyssinians—

GRUMIEL. Shall I cork thee with this mallet?

MOMIEL. Nay, if he will not, let us put a ring in his nose, and haul him along like a bull for the baiting. Nudge him on the other side, with the crank of thy elbow, and see how merrily he'll amble.

ANDREA. O miserable son of a weaver! O unfortunate poet! O intolerably unlucky, and never-enough-to-be-pitied-for-thy-innumerable-and-inexpressible-woes-and-unheard-of-misventures, Andrea della Pimpinella di Ribobolo.

MOMIEL. Ay, ay, that is your *alias;* and like every other knave that would conceal himself, you have as many titles as a Spanish grandee: but it sha'n't serve at this turning : no, no, Signior Alias!

GRUMIEL. Whirl him along, thou accursed stone-chatter! thou soul of a spinster!

ANDREA. I am getting addled as a nest-egg. Am I an animal or a Mameluke?

[*Exeunt the fiends, dragging* ANDREA.

Scene IV.

The dreary halls of the enchanter
Lengthen in antre after antre :
Between the yawning jambs of which
Strong-ribbed portcullises do stretch.
Enormous Powers, on either hand,
Some of the old Titanian band,
With misty eyes and downcast looks
Stand dozing in their hollow nooks,
Club-shapen oaks beneath their arms
To guard the House of Ill from harms :
The dun lords of the feline race
From side to side pass and repass ;
And brinded forms with cruel eyes
Glistening at one another's cries,
Scourge their own sides for ire ; a brood
Kept fierce for war by lack of food
And red repast of luscious blood.
Ten griffins torturing round their stings,
Coil their mail'd lengths in crackling rings,
That ever as their nostrils blow
Sulphury flames, illumined grow,
As if their steely faces shone
With passions, instant come and gone.

See'st thou a funeral canopy
Hang in the black air dismally
Its flaggy curtains?—there doth moan
In easeless sleep the Evil-One:
And there, his painful cockatrice
Lulls him with close incessant hiss,
If lull he may; for Terror still
Keeps him awake against his will.

Upstarts the regal mockery!—now
Flashes the blue spite of his brow,
And now he thrills the batty walls
Of his dull palace, as he calls.

Enter FIENDS.

ARARACH.   No word?—no sign?—no messenger?
Fiends.   None, lord!
ARARACH.   O ye shall freeze, ye slugs! in lakes of
        ice
For this!—ye shall! What! none?—For ages, ay,
Till roaring conflagration seize the world,
Ye shall stand oozing blood from either eye,
With bitter pain!—
Fiends.   Hark! the resounding floors!
Thunders the echoing porch, and clang the barry
        doors!

Enter GRUMIEL *and* MOMIEL, *with* ANDREA
                prisoner.

ARARACH.   What's he? You staring fool! Speak,
        ye torpedos!
Where have ye slept your time?
GRUMIEL.   Master, we bring
Thy victim-rival, the spruce lord—
ARARACH.   That charlatan?—
Ho!—bear these dormice instant to the torture,

Let them be lashed to strips inch-broad ! let both
Trudge blistering o'er a fiery-sanded plain,
While ye on wing do scourge them !

   GRUMIEL. Howl ! howl ! bowl !

   MOMIEL. Ha ! ha !—I care not what I suffer,
      while
I see him get the lashes !—Ha ! ha ! ha ! —
Thou'lt find a springy Oasis in the desert,
Eh, thou discoverer ? or a North Pole
To cool thy feet ?

   GRUMIEL. I'll grind thy head for this,
If ever we get free !

   [*Exeunt* GRUMIEL *and* MOMIEL *with the torturers.*

   ARARACH. Who art thou, idiot ?

   ANDREA. I know no more of my parents, your
worship, than a foundling tied to a knocker. When
I was alive, if I can collect my scattered faculties,
I might, please your worship, have been (without
pride be it spoken !) the only hope of a tailor : but
indeed I have not the boldness to maintain it ; for
within these few minutes, I have, with pure fear
and exaggeration, forgotten all my geography.—Oh,
will these teeth wear themselves round, like a parcel
of jackstones ?—Shall I ever crack a filberd again ?
—Chatter ! chatter ! chatter !

   ARARACH. What have they brought me here ?
      A half-brain'd loon !
A mimmering driveller !—Shove him without !
He's not worth torments. Stáy : thou shalt not go
Without one mark upon thee.—Hence stupidity !
             [*Striking him with his wand.*
Trot on a cloven heel away, and satyr-like,
As Nature should have made thee !—Stretch his ears

F

Into a Panic size !—Go ! scare the wilds,
Thou bungle of a man !—Hoot him away !

    ANDREA. I do most verdantly beseech our Lady
To grant your worship long life and propriety !

[Exit running.

    ARARACH. I'll send these tortured slaves trooping
       again
Upon mine errand : 'twas that yellow fiend
Perplexed his brother. But I'll promise him
Pains that will make his spirit sob to hear them,
If he do so again. I have no choice ;
They are my best of servants. Call those fiends ?

The scene closes.

ACT III.

Scene I.

HE Myrtle Grove :—O gentle Power !
Psyche's aye-blooming bachelor !
Thou in whose curls fell strength abides,
Whose baby hand the lion guides,
I think, with all thy other claims,
Thou'st a sweet choice in very names !
Oft have I dwelt upon thine own ;
LOVE !—'tis a most Æolian tone !
So soft, the lips will scarcely meet,
Almost afraid to fashion it ;
And mark our deepest votaries,—they
Sigh it most silently away !
Was never seen an artless Maid
But smiled to say, or hear it said,
Ev'n though her heart can scarcely tell,
What's in the sound she loves so well :
Was never seen a generous Youth
But vow'd—'twas a sweet word in sooth]
A simple syllable, 'tis true,
Yet born in Heaven like balm and dew ;
In Heaven alone it could have birth,
No child of miserable Earth !
It dropt from the harmonic spheres,
A manna-sound to starving ears.

Name we Love's flowers: The *Rose!* the *Rose!*
Sounds it not queenly as it blows?
And *Lily!*—this is even yet
More inly fine and delicate!—
Thy murmuring bosom-bird, the *Dove,*
Chimes not its name to thine, O Love?
And could the wit of wisest man
Find a much statelier name than *Swan?*—
How many an eye beams slyly coy;
How many a heart trembles with joy;
How many a cheek doth sudden glow;
How many a bosom heaves its snow;
How many a lip, raised in delight,
Just shows the pearl, a line of white;
How many a sigh is breathed, when none
May hear the heart's confession;
How many a throb Hyblœan Love!
Wakes, at these words—*the Myrtle Grove?*
Ay, the pale, wedded, widow'd dame,
Pensive recalls the long-lost name;
A hectic,—one faint wave,—no more!—
Passes her marble beauty o'er;
She smooths the braid upon her brow,
Remembering—Ah! what recks it now?
   Within the grove a bower you see
Of this same lover-loving tree;
Veil'd in its dim recess, and warm,
A Youth still gazes on a form
That stands a-tiptoe, plucking there
Boughs, and green leaves, and blossoms fair:
Wreathing them round her veined wrist,
By none but such entwiner kist,
Our SYLVIA binds, with many a gem
And costly spray, her diadem.

SYLVIA [*Singing as she binds*].
>   Sweet the noise of waters falling,
>   And of bees among the flowers,
>   Wild-birds their companions calling,
>   Summer winds, and summer showers !

This lily ! I must put her next the rose ;
They always go together.

ROMANZO [*Aside*].   Even in rhyme !
SYLVIA.
>   Say, why does that young rose redden ?
>   And why is that lily so pale ?
>   O—she is a new married-maiden,
>   And she—a maid left to wail !

How "left"?—did her lover die ?—It is a song
I've heard my mother sing.—O me ! how soon
This tall Sweet-William faded !—Ay ! 'tis the way !

>   The streams that wind amid the hills,
>   And lost in pleasure slowly roam,
>   While their deep joy the valley fills,—
>   Ev'n these will leave their mountain-home :
>   So may it, love ! with others be,
>   But I will never wend from thee !

>   The leaf forsakes the parent spray,
>   The blossom quits the stem as fast,
>   The rose-enamoured bird will stray,
>   And leave his eglantine at last ;
>   So may it, love ! with others be,
>   But I will never wend from thee !

Come! it is done.   I never weft before
So beautiful a chaplet.
    ROMANZO.   It might wreathe
A brow most godlike !
    SYLVIA.   Ay, and shall do so !
Else I would strew the weeds under my feet,
And break my heart with weeping !

I've pluck'd the wild woodbine, and lilac so pale,
And the sweetest young cowslips that grew in the dale,
The bud from the flower, and the leaf from the tree,
To bind a rich garland, young Shepherd ! for thee.

O look how the rose blushes deeper with pride,
And how pretty forget-me-not peeps by its side ;
How the high-crested pink in brave plumage doth fall,
And look how the lily looks sweeter than all !

My beautiful myrtle !—I think thou dost know
Upon whom this rich garland I mean to bestow ;
For thou seem'st with a voice full of fragrance to sigh—
" Should I wreath that young Shepherd, how happy
    were I ! "

Come, bend me thy brow, gentle youth ! and I'll twine
Round thy temples so pure this rich garland of mine;
O thou look'st such a prince !—from this day, from
    this hour,
I will call thee nought else but the Lord of my Bower !

    ROMANZO.   Would I were so, indeed !—Look ! I
    have knelt
That I may feel thy soft hands in my hair,
Like winds in autumn leaves.   Around thy form

I'll close my suppliant arms, and like a shrine,
Press it to smile on my devotedness !

AGATHA. [*Behind*] 'Tis as I feared ! O these
soft myrtle bowers !

SYLVIA. Now, it is trim as may be. I would keep
Thee ever kneeling thus ; and still would find
Some flower awry to settle : but yon cushat
'Gins her lone widow-note at evening hour ;
That is my warning home !

AGATHA. Still ! still my daughter !

SYLVIA.

   Amid the valleys far away,
  A mother-bird sits on a tree,
   And weeps unto her long-astray—
  " O come my little bird to me !"
   So " long-astray "
   Must now away
   Unto its parent tree !

ROMANZO. A's light the day,
   Or love the May,
   Sweet !—I will follow thee !

AGATHA. They are both innocent : Love's taper
burns
Brightest in purest bosoms.—Yet I'll task him ;
It is a mother's right.—So ! I have met ye !
What a wild pair of ramblers ye have been !—
The whole, whole morn away !

ROMANZO. Nay, we were going
Straight to the cottage ; and the birds' way too,—
The shortest we could see.

AGATHA. Let go my neck,   [*To* SYLVIA.
Thou fondler !—murmuring about my lips
With thy bee kisses. What should I care for thee,
A bird that leaves thy summer-cage, whenc'er
The wicket opens ?

SYLVIA.   Aye, but comes again
To feed upon its mistress' hand, and hide
Its softness in her bosom.
     AGATHA.   There 's no chiding thee !
Hie home; my limbs are weary.   It is time
Our guest should taste refreshment : to prepare it
Has been my morning's work, while you were roam-
          ing.
Go : all is spread ; but still, I think, it wants
Your garnishing : go, deck it with fresh flowers,
As you are wont when we sit all alone.
     SYLVIA.   Then do not ye stay long ! I'll have it
          deckt
Ere ye could pluck the blossoms.   [*Exit.*
     AGATHA.   Sir, your crown
Becomes you bravely !
     ROMANZO.   O it has taken all
Its beauty from the wreather !—her sweet touch
Has lent it a new perfume, and a lustre
It never had before !—Now, she is gone,
I will be king no longer. [*Takes off his crown.*
     AGATHA.   O, sir ! sir !
If you, who are a stranger, can speak thus,
How should another, who has seen this flower
Bud, bloom, and hallow its wild parent-home
With smiles no garden knows !—Forgive me, Youth,
That I speak thus of her : forgive me, too,
This foolish, beating, mother's heart of mine,
That fain would question him who has reveal'd
So much, and yet no more.
     ROMANZO.   I have no secret !
None !—What you ask, I'll answer.—Or, perchance,
You'll hear my life's short story ?   I am a bachelor ;
The lord of some few acres ; whom the love

Of scenes by Nature's wandering pencil drawn,
Has led among these solitudes : with this,
My death, were I to die as I am speaking,
Were all, I ween, that friend or foe could grave
Justly upon my tomb.

AGATHA.   'Tis frankly spoken
And I should mourn to think that Youth had grown
So cunning in the world since I have left it,
To wear a brow so clear as yours, the while
One spot was on the heart.

ROMANZO.   I do confess,
If you would have more witness of my truth
I scarce could give it : being come so far
From Padua, where I studied, and am known,
With but one servant.   He, poor slave, I lost
In the deep gorges of these purple hills
But yesterday.   If we may chance on him,
He will confirm the story you have heard,
And then you must believe.

AGATHA.   I do already :
But still—We mothers !—O, we are such cowards !

ROMANZO.   Put me to trial : I'll submit myself
To a whole year's probation : I will do
Any thing you can ask, if so I may
Win my sweet mistress.—

AGATHA.   Well—well—well
          Re-enter SYLVIA *in terror.*
                              My child !
What ails my love ? my daughter ?

SYLVIA.   Oh ! I have seen
So wild and strange a creature !

ROMANZO.   What ! a wolf?

SYLVIA.   No, some uncouth resemblance of a man,
But not like thee.   As I approach'd the cottage,

From a green nook out-started this rough thing,
And brush'd me swiftly by.   I could not move,
Or cry, with sudden terror ; but stood there
Fixt like a tree, how long I do not know,
Till sense return'd, and scarcely so much strength
As bore me hither.

ROMANZO.   Let it be man or beast
I'll scourge it from this vale !

> [*Tears down a branch, and exit.*

SYLVIA.   O ye kind powers !
Save him, Morgana ! save him !

> [*Exit after* ROMANZO.

AGATHA.   Sylvia !—rash girl !—

> [*Exit after her.*

*The Scene changes to the front of the Cottage, where a
table is laid with refreshments.*

Enter ANDREA.

ANDREA.   *Tin! sin! whee! ree!*—Whether
have been sun-stricken or no, I cannot tell ; bu
my head sings like a boiling kettle.   I think—an
yet I think I don't think.   I remember—and still
I forget what I remember.   Now would I give
natural philosopher, Prato the Grig, or Julia Scissar
of Rome, a very handsome douser if he would ab
solve me whether my feet stand under me, or I stan
under my feet.—Stay : what was I at the time of th
Deluge ?—Oh ! a mandrake, swimming about merrily
and was drowned like the Dutch-skipper with m
hands in my breeches-pockets.   After that I ha
the convoy of a whole fleet of sea-calves, with whic
we peopled the famous Island of Bulls.   I remembe
it as well as my breakfast to-morrow : we multifie
prodigiously there, and should have been lords c

the creation, only that we had some cannibal qualities about us; great beef-eaters! fast-hating fellows!— Hilloah! what's here to be seen? By the mass, here is as soft a carpet of clover as ever I cooled my heels on; good! set that down, commentator! *item:* "an acre of green baize for a sky-coloured parlour." Here, too, is a—Bless me! I totally forget the name for a house—good! no matter; call it a pigeon-box. Finally and firstly of all, I see trenchers to be muncht, and bowls to be quaffed: so will proceed no further in the decalogue, but content myself with this humble shoulder of mutton.

     [*Sits down and helps himself to fruit.*
Admirable!—tastes a little racy or so; it must have had the run of a fruitery. [*Drinking off a bowl of milk.*] Nothing like your creaming Champagne, after all!— Comfort thyself, poor GANDREA! it is now exactly the best part of a fortnight since thou didst swallow a single granary of nutriment. Thou canst not always, man! live upon air, like a camel-leopard.—Sir, you are welcome to Tartary!

  Enter ROMANZO. SYLVIA *and* AGATHA
    following.

 ROMANZO. Who—what art thou that dar'st—
  By all that's strange,
This is my servant, Andrea! but so alter'd
I scarce could know him. Sirrah! where have you
  been,
That you are thus transform'd?
 ANDREA. Indeed I have been spending an hour or two with my old friend, clerk of the kitchen to Ancient Nicolas; so I hope am good company

for any one of the cloth, under a Jesuit or Holy
Inquisitor.

SYLVIA.   It talks strange reason !

AGATHA.   Servant !—O we are lost !
What may the master be, if such the man?

Pray Heaven he be no demon in disguise !

ROMANZO.   Hast thou left off thy reverence with
thy shape ?

Why dost thou not rise up and bow to me ?   Who
am I knave ?

ANDREA.   You?—The man from the moon, I
think, by your crazy appearance.   What a magnifico
you are !   Where's your fur-cloak and your poodle?
—You, indeed !—Orson might have been your great-
aunt by the mother's-side, for all I know of the matter.—Do the people in this quarter dangle such canes
at the wrist as that you are switching your boots
with ?—Oh ! lack-a-day ! lack-a-daisy ! now I remember you !—Let me hear you grumble.

ROMANZO.   Well ! art thou still a stranger to this
frown ?

ANDREA.   Verily I do entertain some oblivious
recollection that I may have seen such a frizziognomy
before : Or is it one from a dream of ugly faces?—
Stop : Odso, now I have it ! You are the bravo that
robbed my unfortunate master, threw him into a mill-
dam hard by, and made me hold my nostril over a
cauldron of deadly night-shade, till I am grown as
dizzy as a beetle.   The same ! I'll swear it before this
Madonna herself !—And these are his very garments,
of which, with sacratitious hands, you have stripped
and deluded his body.   O thief ! burglarer ! fortune-
hunter ! kidnapper !

AGATHA.   What do I hear?

SYLVIA.   There is no truth in him :
Believe not that rude thing !

ANDREA. I'll take it on my. life he is a capital
fellow !—a murderer ! a committer of *fo-paws*, and
every other crime that deserves a halter !—He cannot
deny it !

ROMANZO. Slave ! liar ! devil !
My rage unnerves me !

ANDREA. Will you abscond ?—or must I have you
laid by the heels for a common tax-gatherer?

ROMANZO. Down to the dust, to which I'll crumble
thee !

ANDREA. O, fool ! fool ! fool !—you have demol-
ished at one blow a feast that might have tempted St
Anthony himself !—That pitcher will never recover
the thwack you have given it, if it lived to the age of
Methusalem !—You have injured, O lamentable ! the
rotundity of that cheese beyond redemption ; spoiled
the shape of that pie for ever and long after !—Oons !
he will make a whipt-syllabub of me if I stay any
longer. Roo-roo-roo !

       [Exit pursued by ROMANZO.

  The Scene closes.

Scene II.

 Boots it to tell what all have seen ?
 A Maybush on a village green !
 Its turban'd head with garland wound,
 Its rich skirts spreading on the ground ;
 Like a sultana of the East.
 In all her gay apparel drest.
 Emerald, turkis, ruby rare,
 Beryl, tourmaline are there ;

Pearl, and precious chrysolite,
Sapphire blue, and topaz bright ;
With every gem that ever shone
A Tartar's belt or bonnet on.
But fresher in their different lustres,
Our dew-besprent-festoons, and clusters ;
Purer of tint, and with perfume
Filling wide Nature's boundless room.—
What is a jewel-dropping tree,
O May-bush ! when compared to thee?

———————

STEPHANIA, ROSELLE, JACINTHA, GERONYMO,
and Peasants assembled.

CHORUS.

O May, thou art a merry time,
    Sing hi ! the hawthorn pink and pale !
When hedge-pipes they begin to chime,
    And summer-flowers to sow the dale.

When lasses and their lovers meet
    Beneath the early village thorn,
And to the sound of tabor sweet
    Bid welcome to the Maying-morn !
        O May, thou art; &c.

When gray-beards and their gossips come
    With crutch in hand our sports to see,
And both go tottering, tattling home,
    Topful of wine as well as glee !
        O May, thou art, &c.

But Youth was aye the time for bliss,
    So taste it, Shepherds ! while ye may :
For who can tell that joy like this
    Will come another holiday?
        O May, thou art, &c.

First Peasant. Ha ! ha ! ha !—Now ! who's for ninepins ?

Second Peasant. Who's for ball ?

Third Peasant. I !

Fourth Peasant. And I !

Fifth Peasant. I'm for the bowling-green !

Sixth Peasant. For ball ! for ball !—Pins are only for women and tailors !

GERONYMO. Stay your feet, lads !—and your tongues, ladies !—they are both running without reason. Will you hear me ?

All. Hear him ! hear him ! hear him !

GERONYMO. Plague on't ! You make more noise in keeping silence than the town-criers. Will you stop your bawling ?

All. Ay, stop your bawling ! stop your bawling !

GERONYMO. Mercy upon me, what a set of peace-makers !—Then you will not listen to me ?—You fellow here, with the bull-neck, roar me down these rascals !—only, pray, do not gape so wide, else there is some danger your head may fall off by the ears.

First Peasant. Silence ! Let no man say another word, or I'll make him cry *peccavi !*

GERONYMO. Well said, Hircoles !—you might play Hircoles, without his club, for your fist falls like a weaver's beam.—Now be quiet ! Hear what I have to bring forth ! This it is, lads ; this it is, fellows : or, as it were, this is the tot of the matter ; that is to say, in short and briefly to complain the whole business—We have forgotten to choose a May Queen !—Shall I be heard in this land hereafter ?

All. A May-Queen ! a May-Queen ! who shall we choose ? Who is she to be ? Which is the handsom-est ? And the prettiest ? Ay, and the most beautiful too ? Which is she ?

GERONYMO. Shall I be heard again, I say?

First Peasant. Silence !

GERONYMO. Thanks, thou stertorean fellow !— If Wisdom would be heard she must always keep a swaggerer like this at her elbow. I say, my friends : I humbly repose, that is, I succumb to your better judgments, whether, in this case—mark me 1—thus it stands, or, as I may say, here 'tis : There are so many of these lasses who are the handsomest, and prettiest, ay, and most beautiful one of them all, that I think it would go hard with us to choose her who is the most so. Therefore I humbly assent, and maintain, and suspect, that it is better to let it go by straws.

All. Ay ! ay.! let straws end it !

GERONYMO. Why come then ! see what it is to have a noddle. Here is my hat to hold the lots. Mistress Stephania, a straw for you ; another straw for you, Mistress Roselle ; another, 'nother, 'nother, —straws apiece for the prettiest six among ye. Now listen to me : this is the case, and thus it stands, or as may be delivered in one word, here 'tis : Whoever of ye pulls the longest straw is to be May-Queen. Do I speak like a wiseacre or no?

All. Like a very Salmon ! Spoke like a very Salmon !

Second Peasant. Should we not take the senses of the assembly upon it ?

All. No ! no ! no !—Come, lasses ! draw ! draw ! draw !

STEPHANIA. Very well. [*Pulls a straw.*]

ROSELLE. Ay, very well. [*Pulls.*]

First Girl. [*Pulls.*] O lawk ! such a pudget of a thing !

Second Girl. Now for me ! [*Pulls.*]

Third Girl. [*Pulling.*] I vow I am the longest
of you all !—I vow so it is !

Enter OSME *above, playing on a lyre.*

STEPHANIA.   Hark ! hark ! O hark ! what measures
                play,
              So sweet ! so clear ! yet far away !
ROSELLE.   Whence is the music ? who can say?
JACINTHA.   'Tis like the crystal sound of wells,
              Betrampled by the sparkling rain !
STEPHANIA.   Or dew-drops fall'n on silver bells
              That tingle o'er and o'er again !
First Girl.   'Tis in the air !
Second Girl.   'Tis underground !
Third Girl.   'Tis everywhere !
Fourth Girl.   The magic sound !
All.   Hush ! O hush ! and let us hear :
            'Tis too beautiful to fear.

OSME *sings and plays.*

Hither ! hither !
O come hither !
Lads and lasses come and see !
Trip it neatly,
Foot it featly,
O'er the grassy turf to me !

There are bowers
Hung with flowers,
Richly curtain'd halls for you !
Meads for rovers
Shades for lovers,
Violet beds, and pillows too !

G

Purple heather
You may gather
Sandal-deep in seas of bloom !
Pale-faced lily,
Proud Sweet-Willy,
Gorgeous rose, and golden broom ?

Odorous blossoms
For sweet bosoms,
Garlands green to bind the hair ;
Crowns and kirtles
Weft of myrtles,
Youth may choose, and Beauty wear !

Brightsome glasses
For bright faces
Shine in ev'ry rill that flows ;
Every minute
You look in it
Still more bright your beauty grows !

Banks for sleeping,
Nooks for peeping,
Glades for dancing, smooth and fine !
Fruits delicious
For who wishes,
Nectar, dew, and honey-wine !

Hither ! hither !
O come hither !
Lads and lasses come and see !
Trip it neatly,
Foot it featly,
O'er the grassy turf to me !

[*Exeunt Peasants led by the music.*

Scene III.

A bosky woodland near the bounds
Of Queen Morgana's sunny grounds.
Under a spreading maple tree
Sits a rude Swain, as rude may be,
With canes, and marsh flags on his knee ;
Seven hollow pipes his artless hands
Strive to conjoin with rushy bands ;
And with a grave, yet smirking air,
He trolls satyric ditties there,
Forgetful of the form he wore,
And almost all he was before.

ANDREA. I have grown wondrous 'rithmetical of
late, being, indeed, most lamentably given to poesy
and numbers.   But chiefly of all I affect the pastoral,
the *fal-lal*, or as it may be very opprobriously
described,—the lambkin style of farcification.   Let
me see : what can I do in this way ?

'Tis sweet among the purling groves
    To sit in sunny shade,
And hear the frisky turtle-doves
    Skip o'er the 'namelled glade.
        The amorous sheep go coo-oo !
        The birds go baa-aa too !
        And I upon my crook do play
        While o'er the fields I take my—steps !

The dappled daisy—No !—
    When hairy morn—Pize on't !—
Where meadows full of fishes be,
    And streams with daisies dight,

My dappled goats do pipe to me
From Night to airy Morn.
   The fragrant goats sing faa-laa,
   The Shepherd he goes maa-aa !
Till both are tired of food and play,
And then he drives his flock astray.

Such is the peaceful Shepherd's strife—

And here be two of his black sheep—

Enter GRUMIEL *and* MOMIEL.

MOMIEL. Didst thou not mark them winding
   down the glen
Flaunting their quickset crowns?
  GRUMIEL.   Ay, what of that?
  MOMIEL. What of it? humph !—this fellow hunts
   as keen
As a blind grayhound ; cannot scent his prey
Though rubb'd to 's nose.
  GRUMIEL.   What 's to be made of clowns
And country-queans?
  MOMIEL.   Ingenious Mischief turns
The clumsiest tools into brave instruments
When work is to be done.   Leave all to me :
I 'll save thy back a drubbing.—Ho ! thou knave !
  ANDREA. The same to you, sir ; and may you
long deserve the title !
  MOMIEL. Put on this ivy skirt, this gown of leaves
To hide thy shaggy limbs : and here !—this too—
This bulrush bonnet, that thy horns and ears
May perk not out.
  ANDREA. It fits me like a bee hive, or an old hat
on a broomstick, to fright crows in a corn-field.
What a farthingale too !—Now if I were only simple

enough, I might pass for a wild Indianness, and exhibit myself as a pattern of unsophisticated nature.

MOMIEL.   Listen to me dull beast !—Thou hast
  but smell'd
The oblivious liquor, yet art drunk as though
Thou hadst been soak'd in it.   Hear what I say,
And what thou hast to do.   If thou forget'st it,
I 'll bend four pines to earth, whose strong recoil
Shall fling thee piece-meal o'er their whistling backs
To where the great winds rise !

ANDREA.   Sir, I will not regret a tittle of it, if it
were even as long and tedious as a curtain-lecture to
a tired courier.

MOMIEL.   Thou wert best not.   Come hither to
  this knoll ;
See'st thou yon troop of villagers ?

ANDREA.   I do.

MOMIEL.   They 're seeking a May-Qneen : dost
  hear.

ANDREA.   Why, ay,
Catching May-flies you say.

MOMIEL.   A May-Queen, fool !
           [*Strikes him.*

GRUMIEL.   Good ! rap it into his skull !

MOMIEL.   What was 't I said ?

ANDREA.   Eh ?—Oh !—Ay !   catching a May-
  Queen.

MOMIEL.   So !—well !—
Thou hast no more to do, but take this wreath
And cast it in their path.   Dost hear me, idiot ?

ANDREA.   With my two eyes.

MOMIEL.   Begone then, to thy service !
Look thou perform it, or I'll strangle thee !
      [*Exeunt* GRUMIEL *and* MOMIEL.

ANDREA. Fear not; I will do it most ingenuously.

The Scene changes to another part of the Glen.

Enter the Peasants.

ROSELLE. This will-o'-the-wisp of a musician hath stopt in time; I am weary almost to fainting. Proceed, neighbours; I must sit down a moment on this bank.

STEPHANIA. Nay, I will bear you company. Go on, friends; we'll follow you towards the cottage, when my sister is able to walk.

Peasants. Very well. Trudge on, Geronymo. You are the head gander in this wild goose exhibition.   [*Exeunt Peasants.*

The Scene changes again.

Enter the Peasants.

GERONYMO. Where are we now, can any body tell?

Second Peasant. In a maze, that's certain.

GERONYMO. Thank ye, for the discovery: What a treasure thou would'st be to a map-maker!

Third Peasant. We are all astray, like the Babes in the Wood, and therefore I see nothing better we can do but innocently sit down upon the ground, and kiss one-another.

GERONYMO. Stay; who's there?—Hollo! neighbour in the green petticoat; a word with ye!

Enter ANDREA.

First Girl. Lawk! such a fright!

Second Girl. Prithee, good woman, from what pedlar do you buy your millinery?

GERONYMO. I remember seeing such another face

upon a city-fountain, with a cap of reeds like a floating island.

First Peasant. Haw ! haw ! haw ! haw !—'A looks as if 'a was carrying off a bed of turnips !—haw ! haw ! haw ! haw !

Third Peasant. Excellent !—Or crying jonquils by the hundred !

Fourth Peasant. Who are you !—Whence come you ?—What 's your business ?

ANDREA. 'T is more easily told than yours to ask it. But no matter : Stand round, and I will unlighten you with a clear exploration.

Fifth Peasant. I 'll warrant you she 's a basket-maker, by these rushes.

All. Well ? — What is't ? — Speak ! — Now !— Begin !—Out with 't !

ANDREA. Why then, if you will know, the long and the short of the matter is this, *videlicet* : I am come to elect myself unanimously your May-Queen !

All. A May-Queen ! ha ! ha ! ha !—You a May-Queen !—O good !—O the monster !—

ANDREA. Monster !—do ye select me for a monster ?—Perchance there are others in the company who have as good a right to the honour, if there were a fair show of horns for it. But here ! ye ungrateful plebeians ! take this halter—[*throwing down the wreath*] and hang yourselves in it, *verbatim et literatim* every one of ye ! I have done with such vagabonds !   [*Exit, but returns.*

Fifth Peasant. I knew she was a weaver of some sort or other, by her pestilent tongue ?

First Girl. Lawk ! what is this ?
                    [*Taking up the wreath.*

Second Girl. O beautiful !

Third Girl.   Let me see it !

Fourth Girl.   We 'll all see it ?—let it go round !

Fifth Girl.   What a precious—Lo ! here's a scroll, too, stuck in the middle !—Where is Jacintha ?—She is a scholar—Let her read the intents of it.   She can say her *a, b, ab,* as quick as nobody.

JACINTH.   [*Reads.*]

> This wreath by fairy fingers twined,
> One brow, and one alone, will bind:
> Her whom it suits let all obey,
> And choose her as their Queen of May.

First Girl.   Lawk ! I'm sure it will just fit me : it is just my size.

[*Puts on the wreath, which enlarges and falls about
her on the ground.*

ANDREA.   By Saint Bridget, then, you must be just the cut of a landlady !

Second Girl.   Let me try it !

[*It contracts to a single tuft on her head.*

ANDREA.   She wears it as a hen sparrow does her topping.   It will come to me after all !

[*The Girls all try it, but without success.*

All.   Nay, we must look farther.   Where is Stephania?   Where is Roselle ?—Here they come ! Show it ! give it them !

Enter STEPHANIA, *and* ROSELLE.

Fourth Girl.   Whoever this fits is to be May-Queen.   'T is a fairy garland.   Read here !

STEPHANIA.   [*Trying it.*]   Pooh ! it has slipt off me—

ANDREA.   Like a cat down a cottage-eave !

ROSELLE.   Then it must be mine !—Come ! I'll be chaired ! [*Trying it on.*]   Plague on 't ! 't is be-witched !   I 'll none of it.

ANDREA. Well said, Mistress Magnanimity.

STEPHANIA. Where did ye get it?

ROSELLE. How did you come by it?

GERONYMO. Why, let me speak—here 't is : From this smooth cheeked damsel before ye ; this Water-goddess !

STEPHANIA. As sure as sure, I see our friend Andrea in disguise ! hid beneath these flags and rushes, like Love amongst the Roses ! 'T is he ! What say you, Roselle?

ROSELLE. I would almost swear to that leering eye of his, with the crow's-foot stepping into it ! But he has grown as barbarous as an ape since we last saw him. It is ! it is the self-same gentleman ! Does he come in this habit to frighten us? Hang him, scare-crow.

GERONYMO. An imposthume? An imposthume ! He is an imposthume, neighbours !

All. Ho ! a wolf in sheep's clothing !—Tear off his rushy cap there ! Off with it !

[*They pull off his cap.*

STEPHANIA *and* ROSELLE. Ah !—Save us ! deliver us !

ANDREA. What is the matter with the gipsies ?—Do they take me for the ghost of some young man whom they have seduced to commit homicide ?

ROSELLE. O now indeed unhappy Signior Pimplenose !

STEPHANIA. Miserable Ribobolo ! Mercy upon us ! what a pair of ears he has got !

ANDREA. Why, what fault have you with my ears, little Mistress Red Riding-Hood ?—Am I going to swallow you ?

STEPHANIA. What new mishap has overtaken

you?—Have you been in the pillory since we saw
you, that your ears are stretched to such a size?
Have you been hectoring in a tap-room, and been
pulled out by the ears, that they are lengthened so
prodigiously?

ANDREA.   Prodigiously!—Why, what would you
have of them?—I'm sure they are better than those
half-crown pieces of yours with holes punched i' the
middle! You have no more ears than a fish! Methinks it is ye who have been in the pillory, and have
had your ears cropt for perjury, like a holly-bush.
Show me any beast upon earth but yourselves with
such apologies for sound-catchers, and I'll pare mine
down to the heel like an old cheese.—No! these,
indeed, are something like ears! these are respectable
hearing-leathers!   But yours!— I would as soon
think of listening through a couple of penny whistles!
—Perchance you will say my horns, too, are a little
branchy or so?

STEPHANIA.   Horrible! horrible!

ROSELLE.   *Ave Maria! santa purissima!*

GERONYMO.   *Et secula seculorum!*—O for a priest
to conjure him!

ANDREA.   Well, come, this is good now! as if
they never saw horns before!

STEPHANIA.   Never on you! never on you! D'ye
think I'd keep company with a rhinoceros?

ROSELLE.   Some wicked fairy has charmed him
into this shape! he is enchanted!

ANDREA.   Charming and enchanting!—Why ay,
they always said these ornaments became me.

ROSELLE.   O dreadful!—had you these budders
when we knew you at the mill?

ANDREA.   These?—Bless you, I should take cold

without them !—I never was without horns in my
life ! I was born with them, like a young snail. My
horns and ears grew together, one behind the other,
like mushrooms.

ROSELLE. Nay, 'tis false ! you had them not !—
we should have seen them !

ANDREA. O effrontery ! what will the world come
to at last ?—They will begin to persuade me just now
that I never wore hooves either ; but that these feet
are no better than theirs, letter L's turned under
them.— *[Showing his feet.*

Peasants. The devil ! the devil in a bottle-green
petticoat !—Fly, neigbours ! run for it, countrymen !
—Off ! off !—Let us break our own necks rather than
be eaten alive by this goat-footed heretic !
[They run away.

ANDREA. As I 'm a person, I never saw such ill-
bred people in my life !—They were never at court,
as I was, that 's plain as the face upon my nose !—
Let them die in their simplicity, ignorants !—I wash
their hands of me for ever ! *[Exit.*

Scene IV.

Lost in a fit of meditation
ROMANZO takes his sullen station
Fast by a rock, from which a stream
Tumbles its little waves of cream
Into a basin, whence it wells
Clearly and calmly through the dells.
The spot is lone, I grant, but then
So is the whole Enchanted Glen ;
And though our Youth would seem to roam,—
'T is not ten steps from Sylvia's home.

ROMANZO.   Her mother shuns me, and with eyes
      averse,
Hardly endures my sight.   What she may think,
I cannot tell ; but that denial strange
Of my fool servant, gave her cautious nature
Reason to doubt I am not what I say.
Yet I will not forsake them :—Some dark storm
Seems to make heavy the dull air about us,
Although the sky is clear.   I 'll see it down ;
Perchance I may have leave, if it do come,
To stand between the thunder-bolt and them :
This is a hope !—My Sylvia, too, is kind,
Still kind ! and with yet dearer, sweeter smiles,
Endeavours to repair her mother's frowns.—
What noise is here ?

Enter the Peasants.

Some villagers a-maying : Who are ye ?
      GERONYMO.   Why here 't is, your worship :   We
are the most harmful people in the world ; and
indeed would not tread upon a worm if it sought our
mercy.   Yet have we been assailed here in this wood,
by—saving your worship's worship !—no less a per-
sonage than Satan himself, in the form of a mountain-
goat, only that he stood on 's hind legs, bolt upright ;
with eyes like two red-hot warming-pans, ten horns,
each as tall as a young oak-tree, and whisking a long
tail over his head as if he was going to thrash us with
it.—In short—
      ROMANZO.   Be you at peace !—I have expell'd him
      hence.
It is no devil, but a mortal wretch
Whom the elves sport with, and have thus trans-
      form'd,
To make them merriment.

GERONYMO. We humbly thank your worship for exercising him from this place. Can your worship detect us to a little green cottage, that bubbles over the stream somewhere here about?

ROMANZO. Here come the owners ; they will best direct you. [*Retires.*

GERONYMO. A very personable sort of person, I 'll assure ye, for a person of these parts !—O lud ! here is a most preternatural creature !

Enter SYLVIA, *and* AGATHA.

Peasants. Huzza ! huzza !—This is she ! This is she whom we have been looking for !—Not such a beauty in all the Earth, nor in the New World either ! —Welcome to our Queen ! welcome ! welcome !— Huzza !

SYLVIA. Good people ! wherefore do ye come
    with shouts
To break the holy silence of this vale ?
Would ye aught with us ?

Peasants. To it, Geronymo !

SYLVIA. Why do you call me "Queen"? and
    throw your wreaths
At my unworthy feet ?—By my simplicity !
I do not love the title !

Peasants. Plague on 't ! will nobody out with a speech?—I could as soon look at the sun in his brightness !—My tongue cleaves to the roof of my mouth, like the hammer to an old bell !—She 's a rare pretty one, that's certain !—Geronymo ! where is thy 'ration?— Where have we lived that we have never seen her before ?—Geronymo ! plague take him, where is his speech? where is his 'ration ?—Begin ! I 'll second thee, man ! I 'll stand behind thee !

GERONYMO.   Most mightiful ! and most beautiful !
and most dutiful princess ! We do most passionately
design and request that—And—so—hum !—that—
hem !—In a word, and as I may say, thus it stands,
or here 't is, most lovely flower of this flowery loveliness ! We have been tickled hither in the ear by an
indivisible singing-bird, through dangers and demons,
over precipices and watercresses, in spite of quagmires
and quicksands, by numberless out-of-the-way short-
cuts, and straight-forward roundabouts, from our
village to this place—

Peasants.   Bravo ! bravo !

GERONYMO.   Mar me not ! I am in the very
passion of it !—And so, to include my narration, thou
paradox of beauty ? thou superlatively superexcellent
and most sweet creature ! we come in a body to offer
you our loves and submissions ; for 't is only looking
at your pretty face for one moment to see that you,
and none but you, are she whom Destiny has cut out
with her shears for our May-Queen !

Peasants.   Huzza !—the wreath ! the wreath !—
Crown her !—Huzza !

SYLVIA *is crowned as May-Queen.*

SYLVIA.   'T is all so sudden that I cannot strive—
Nay, choose some other—It will not become—

AGATHA.   Would every crown were worn as
      peacefully !

SYLVIA *is carried by the Peasants to a flowery bank
where she is installed as May-Queen.*

Peasants.   The song ! the song that our pastor
taught us for the 'casion !—Come ?—the roundel ! the
roundel !—Take hands, and sing it as we dance
about and about her.

There's a bank with rich cowslips, and cuckoo-buds
 strewn,
  To exalt your bright looks, gentle Queen of the
   May;
Here's a cushion of moss for your delicate shoon,
 And a woodbine to weave you a canopy gay!

Here's a garland of red maiden-roses for you,
 Such a beautiful wreath is for beauty alone!
Here's a golden king-cup, brimming over with dew,
 To be kiss'd by a lip just as sweet as its own!

Here are bracelets of pearl from the fount in the dale,
 That the Nymph of the wave on your wrists doth
  bestow;
Here's a lily-wrought scarf, your sweet blushes to
 veil,
  Or to lie on that bosom like snow upon snow!

Here's a myrtle enwreath'd with a jessamine band,
 To express the fond twining of Beauty and Youth:
Take this emblem of love in thy exquisite hand,
 And do THOU sway the evergreen sceptre of Truth!

Then around you we'll dance, and around you we'll
 sing!
  To soft pipe, and sweet tabor we'll foot it away!
And the hills, and the vales, and the forests shall
 ring
  While we hail you our lovely young Queen of the
   May!

GERONYMO. I am taken! I am quite taken!—

Venus, the God of Love, has shot me through the breast with his quiver! My heart falls asunder like a cleft apple!—Madam Agatha, I would have some words with you.

AGATHA. With me, friend?

GERONYMO. Ay, Madam.—Now to break the ice in delicate manner!—You must know, Madam; the case is thus, or thus it stands, or in other terms and insinuations, here 't is, and this is the tot of the matter: I am over head and ears with Mistress Sylvia, your daughter—in short, I love her to destruction—and so, if your politics happen to suit, I hope we shall have your dissent to our marriage.

AGATHA. (*Aside.*) What should I say now?—My mind misgives me about this Traveller, as he calls himself: and even were he what he pretends, is he a fit husband for my lowly daughter? This honest villager would make my Sylvia a homelier, but perchance a happier mate.

GERONYMO. Well?—What say you, Madam Quietly?

AGATHA. How now? What is the matter?

SYLVIA. O me! a heavy slumber seals mine eyes!
Vapours as thick as Night curtain me round
With herse-like folds; and the moist hand of Death
Laid coldly on my brow presses me down
Upon the dreary pillow of Oblivion.
Mother!—where art thou? Fare thee well, my love!
Good-night for ever!—ever!—

AGATHA. Alas! what strange disorder?—These changes and surprises have wrought too much upon her tenderness. Bear her within, my friends, to her green chamber. This way—gently—so—

[*She is borne in.*

Second Peasant. This joy hath a sorrowful ending. Let us go home, and return to-morrow by daylight to enquire after her.

Peasants. Let us do so. Alas ! poor maiden !

[*Exeunt.*

GERONYMO. Marry, I 'll not stir a foot ! I 'll wait, Heaven willing ! though 't were a thousand years : that I 'm dissolved upon !

STEPHANIA. Ho ! ho ! my weathercock is inconstant, I see. But he shall not shift his tail without a breeze, or I 'm no daughter of a true woman ! So, Mister Geronymo ! you are going to——

GERONYMO. I am, incontinently. [*Exit.*

ROSELLE. Follow him, sister; follow him. We 'll give him no more peace than a kettle at a dog's tail. We 'll make him wish himself deaf and us dumb ; we 'll speak knitting-needles into his ear, till his head grows all miz-miz and infusion.

STEPHANIA. The ungrateful fellow !—After all my pains to tangle him !

ROSELLE. The saucy jackanapes, rather ! Come ! he shall neither eat, drink, nor be merry, with any comfort, till he gives us satisfaction : We too can be dissolved upon this matter. Follow me !

[*Exeunt.*

Scene V.

Within the Sorcerer's dread domain
Behold poor ANDREA again !
Hither the wily fiends decoyed him ;
Being too simple to avoid 'em.
Whatever more beseems you know,
The characters themselves will show.

H

GRUMIEL, MOMIEL, *and* ANDREA.

GRUMIEL.   Well, brain-spinner !
What fly is this fine web of thine to catch ?
Plague on thy sleights and stratagems ! ne'er used
But when the arm lacks power.—Deeds ! deeds !
    deeds !
'T is sleight of hand that suits me best !
    MOMIEL.   Tall soul !—
Where'er he comes are blows, and blows enough ;—
But then he gets them ; that he calls his courage !
If courage were esteemed by what it bears
No Pantaloon were ever half so valiant,
For he stands kicks like compliments ; and bangs
Too hard for Punchinello's wooden cheek.
He takes like fan-taps, ladies' punishment !—
I 'll no such courage !
    GRUMIEL.   Well ? what mutter'st thou ?
    MOMIEL.   Let me work on, I tell thee, or thou 'lt
rue it :
Spoil me this scheme and I 'll undo thy doings !—
Come hither, block !   [*To* ANDREA.
              Stoop down, and hold thy head
Under this weed I wring : the juice of it
Dropt in the winding channel of thine ear
Will reach the brain, and like a chymic drug
Precipitate the thick and muddy film
That now hangs dully, as a cloud in air,
Between the light and sense.   Be thou again
The natural fool we found thee, but no more !
    ANDREA.   Thank ye, most considerate gentlemen !
—ye do not pinch my collar so wofully as at first.
As I'm a person ! it shall do ye no disservice.   Come !
speak the word ; if ye are ambitious for office, say
it !   I will recommend ye as the most tender-hearted

catchpolls : the most worthy to be thief-catchers and bumbailiffs, that any honest man would like to have to do withal.

MOMIEL. Peace, gabbler !—Look at thy feet !

ANDREA. O marvellous !

MOMIEL. Stoop o'er this green reflector, and behold

Within its shivering mirror, what thou art.

Wilt bend, and kiss thine image?

ANDREA. That's not me !

Eh?—let me feel !—'Tis true !—O lack ! O transmigration ! Why my own father, wise as he is, would not know me again !—When did these sprouts put forth ?— I am furnished like a two-year old buffalo !—they will slay me shortly for my hide and horns !—There is enough upon my head to set up a dozen dealers in tortoise - shell combs and knife-handles :—Ears too, into which you might thrust your hands like hedging-gloves !—O lamentable ! lamentable !

GRUMIEL. Knock him o' the head !

MOMIEL. No !—Listen, thou wretch :

Our art which has deformed thee, can re-form

As easily. But thou must earn with pains

Thy disenthralment from this bestial shape.

Wilt thou, on promise to be re-made man—

ANDREA. I will !—Turn out your Ogres and your Green Dragons ; I'll put them to flight like crows !— Where be these Anthropophagi ?—Show 'em to me ! —Anything but the old Lady of Babylon herself, I'll undertake for ; and even with her too, I would venture to cross a horn !—Give me a cudgel, if you love me ! and let me be doing—

GRUMIEL. (*Strikes him*). There !—is 't not a tough one? eh?

ANDREA.   This is giving me the cudgel with a
vengeance !—He is an orator, I suppose, and speaks
to the feelings ! an indelible-impression-leaver, hang
him !

MOMIEL.   Wilt not have done ?
I'll crack thy neck if thou speak'st one more word !—
List what I say : Follow this creeping stream
And it will lead thee to a hut, where live
An old dame and her daughter.   Live, I say,
Though now I guess thou'lt find the younger one
Laid on a flowery bier, with doleful clowns
Trooping around it.   Her thou must contrive
To bear off hitherward ; and fetch her safe
To where I will appoint.   Do this but featly
And thou shalt be restored by our great Art,
To thy old shape.   What answer ?   Is 't agreed ?

ANDREA.   Say no more !—I will carry her off as
a lion does a lamb.   What ! did I not belong to the
honourable fraternity of conveyancers ?—Did I not
lie for a whole summer, among the Lazzaroni, on the
steps of the Transport Office, at Naples ? She shall be
translated hither as softly as a bishop to a new bene-
fice ; as dexterously as if I had served an apprentice-
ship to an undertaker, or been purveyor to an anato-
mist.   There are, to be sure, sweeter occupations
under the moon than body-snatching ; but the old
proverb sanctifies it, on this occasion, for " Needs
must "—the rest might be personal—Mum !

MOMIEL.   Come, we will show thee where we 'll
             take our stand,
To watch thy enterprise, and see the issue,
That we may give, receiving ; or perchance,
If need be, to rush out and help thy weakness.
Follow the clue I gave thee : we 'll be near.
                                        [*Exeunt.*

ACT IV.

Scene I.

MORNING: I would but cannot sing
How with light foot, and half-spread
    wing,—
Or as a lady-page that soothes
A steed whose neck she hardly smoothes,
While proud, yet mad, to be carest,
He turns his red eye on her breast,
Snorts with high rage, yet stoops his crest —
Day's bright conductress in doth come
Sleeking two coursers pied with foam,
And her white clasp their bridles on,
Leads in the chariot of the Sun.
Enough to say that Morn appears,
When smiles may turn so soon to tears.
How know I there's no cause to weep?
What meant that fatal cloud of sleep?
In yonder bower my SYLVIA lies,
O that the gentle girl would rise.
Glad my fond heart, and greet mine eyes!—
Come in, come in, thou loitering lover!
I burn till this suspense be over.

Enter ROMANZO.

ROMANZO.   The dawn springs, yet no day-light to
    my soul !—
Soft ! I will wake this bird, whose heavenly song
Cheers all beneath it.   She was wont to pour
Her morning salutation to the sun,
From peaked hill, ere he had tipt with light,
The watery lamps that hang upon the thorn,
Or tinged their crystals blue.   Come, let me wake
    her
With a lark's call !—

    Awake thee, my Lady-love !
      Wake thee, and rise !
    The sun through the bower peeps
      Into thine eyes !

    Behold how the early lark
      Springs from the corn !
    Hark, hark how the flower-bird
      Winds her wee born !

    The swallow's glad shriek is heard
      All through the air !
    The stock-dove is murmuring
      Loud as she dare !

    Apollo's wing'd bugleman
      Cannot contain,
    But peals his loud trumpet-call
      Once and again !

    Then wake thee, my Lady-love !
      Bird of my bower !
    The sweetest and sleepiest
      Bird at this hour !

No stir ?—no word ?—what should this silence be ?—
O she is dead i' the night !—Sylvia ! What, Sylvia !
Away, false ceremony ! I 'll enter here !

> [*Bursts in through the lattice door of* SYLVIA'S
> *chamber.*

Enter AGATHA *from the door of the cottage.*

AGATHA.   Alas ! what noise was that ?—
   My child !—Geronymo !—
Help ! help !—Some villain—

> [*Exit into* SYLVIA'S *chamber through the lattice door.*

Enter ROMANZO *from the cottage door, with the body
   of* SYLVIA *in his arms.* GERONYMO, STE-
   PHANIA, ROSELLE, JACINTHA, *and the other
   Peasants.*

ROMANZO.   Peace, good woman ! peace !—
She sleeps like marble on a monument,
As cold and soundly—But not dead !—not dead !—
No ! no !—Else that firm-propp'd, high-fixed ocean
Pendant above us, would melt o'er our heads,
And drown the miserable sight in tears !—
O, what will come of this ?

AGATHA.   [*From the cottage door.*]   Where has he
   ta'en her ?

ROMANZO.   I sought you, painfully. Away ! away !
You shall not have her now.   Hark ! was she sighing ?

GERONYMO.   Alack, she 's dead ! stark dead !

ROMANZO.   Thou slanderous liar !
But for this precious burden in my arms,
I 'd teach thee croak—

AGATHA.   Sylvia —She 's gone ?—she 's dead !—
She stirs not !—breathes not ! —

ROMANZO.   Dead ?

GERONYMO.   Aye, dead as clay !

ROMANZO.   Is it e'en so?—Why, then, I do
    beseech ye
That we may both be buried in one grave!
    AGATHA.   O he has murder'd her!—he has
    disgraced
My child, and then destroy'd her!
    Peasants.   Villain! villain!
    GERONYMO.   Down with him! down with him!
Drive him away!   Off! off!

                    [*The Peasants assault* ROMANZO.
    ROMANZO.   O use your will! my pride of man is
    o'er!
If all your staves were straws, I could not face them!
                    [*Exit, the Peasants following.*

AGATHA, STEPHANIA, *and* ROSELLE *bear* SYLVIA
    to the cottage.

The Scene closes.

Scene II.

Deep in a wild sequester'd nook,
Where Phebus casts no scorching look,
But Earth's soft carpet moist and green,
Freckled with golden spots is seen;
Where with the wind that swayeth him
The pine spins slowly round his stem;
The willow weeps as in despair
Amid her green dishevelled hair;
And long-arm'd elms, and beeches hoar,
Spread a huge vault of umbrage o'er:
Yet not so thick but yellow day
Makes through the leaves his splendid way;
And though in solemness of shade,

The place is silent, but not sad ;
Here as the Naiad of the spring
Tunes her deep-sounding liquid string,
And o'er the streamlet steals her song,
Leading its sleepy waves along,—
How rich to lay your limbs at ease
Under the humming trellises,
Bow'd down with clustering blooms and bees !
And leaning o'er some antique root
Murmur as old a ditty out,
To suit the low incessant roar,
The echo of some distant shore,
Where the sweet-bubbling waters run
To spread their foamy tippets on :
Or mid the dim green forest aisles
Still haughtier than cathedral piles,
Enwrapt in a fine horror stand
Musing upon the darkness grand.
Now looking sideways through the glooms
At ivied trunks shap'd into tombs ;
Now up the pillaring larches bare
Arching their Gothic boughs in air :
Perchance you wander on, in pain
To catch green glimpses of the plain,
Half glad to see the light again !
And wading through the seeded grass
Out to a sultry knoll you pass ;
There with cross'd arms, in moral mood,
Dreadless admire the cloister'd wood,
Returning your enhancèd frown,
Darker than night, stiller than stone.

But now the Sun with dubious eye
Measures the downfall of the sky,
And pauses, trembling, on thy brow,

Olympus, ere he plunge below
Where ever-thundering Ocean lies
Spread out in blue immensities.
No stir the forest dames among,
No aspen wags a leafy tongue,
Absorb'd in meditation stands
The cypress with her swathed hands,
And even the restless Turin-tree
Seems lost in a like reverie ;
Zephyr hath shut his scented mouth,
And not a cloud moves from the south ;
The hoary thistle keeps his beard,
Chin-deep amid the sea-green sward,
And sleeps unbrushed by any wing
Save of that gaudy flickering thing
Too light to wake the blue-hair'd king :
Alone of the bright-coated crowd
This vanity is seen abroad,
Sunning his ashy pinions still
On flowery bank or ferny hill :
Now not a sole wood-note is heard,
The wild reed breathes no trumpet-word,
Ev'n the home-happy cushat quells
Her note of comfort in the dells ;—
'Tis Noon !—and in the shadows warm
You only hear the gray flies-swarm,
You gaze between the earth and sky,
With wide, unconscious, dizzy eye,
And like the listless willow seem
Dropping yourself into a dream.

But look !—who rides before you now,
Light cavalier ! upon a bough ?—
Awake, and hear the merry elf
Say what he comes about himself.

NEPHON *astride upon an elm-branch swinging himself
up and down.*

Heigh ho ! heigh ho !
Ponderous as the fleecy snow,
Up and down, and up I go !
I can raise a storm, I trow !—
Pumping up the air below
Off the branch myself I blow !

[*Descends.*

O who is so merry, so merry, heigh ho !
As the light-hearted fairy, heigh ho !
He dances and sings
To the sound of his wings,
With a hey, and a heigh, and a ho !

O who is so merry, so airy, heigh ho !
As the light-headed fairy, heigh ho !
His nectar he sips
From the primrose's lips,
With a hey, and a heigh, and a ho !

O who is so merry, so wary, heigh ho !
As the light-footed fairy, heigh ho !
His night is the noon,
And his sun is the moon.
With a hey, and a heigh, and a ho !

But I, forsooth, must work by day
Because I am a cunning fay !
'Ads me ! I 'm sorry I 'm so clever,
Else I had nought to do for ever,
But mingle with the moon-light elves,
That catch the spray on river shelves,

For snowballs to bepelt each other,
Or deep in pearly tombs to smother.
Ah, Nephon ! but the queen, you know,
Calls you her blithe and dapper beau,
You must not scorn her service so.
    Hem ! Hum !—let me see !—
    What is my first deed to be ?—
Here I take my chair of state
Underneath this sunflower great ;
Now I cock my arms, and frown
Like village-beadle in blue gown ;
Now I stroke my beard, and now
Wrinkle deep my sapient brow,
That I may appear to be
Lost in my own profundity.—
Ay ; we have matters grave to do :
So with a short corant, or two,
Ere I begin,—around yon flower,
I 'll sing a span-new sonnet o 'er

    Pretty lily ! pretty lily !
      Why are you so pale ?
    Why so fond of lone-abiding
      Ever in a vale ?

    Pretty lily ! pretty lily !
      Are you lover-lorn ?
    That you stand so droopy-headed,
      Weeping night and morn.

[*A voice from the flower.*]
    Idle fairy ! idle fairy !
      Prattle here no more,
    But be gone, and do your bidding
      As you should before.

NEPHON.   Ha?—ha?—that's Osmé!—Come,
    I know your voice;
It is the sweetest of our tribe:—Come forth;
You need not hide within that flowery bell,
Nor think to cheat me; come, I know you well.

    OSME.   [*Coming out of the lily.*]
Nephon, the queen is angry that you stay,
And sent me down to bid you haste away.
Two fiends are coming; dark, malignant things!
List! you may hear the brushing of their wings
Along the distant grass.—Away, dear Nephon!

    NEPHON.   Off! off! off!
Like a needle of light from the sun
So straight to my object I run!   [*They vanish.*

Scene III.

Within the Vale, a little vale
Strew'd with its own sweet flowers pale;
And made by deep surrounding hill
More lonely, yet more lovely still.

    Were a high-raised and hoary stone,
Cross-crown'd, a tomb, itself alone,—
I'd think yon mossy rock and gray
Were ev'n the very thing I say:
Were two green willows bending o'er
A stone, and seeming to deplore,
Proof that a slumberer lay beneath
Clasped to the icy cheek of Death,—
I'd think yon willows surely wept
Some one in that cold dalliance kept:—
Were garlands white, on willows hung,
Sign that one died, and died too young,

Changing the light robe for the pall,
The bridal for the funeral,—
Yon pallid wreaths would make me fear
Some Flower of Youth lay buried here :
Were yews, green-darkling in their bloom,
Sentinels only of the tomb,—
Were cypress-mourners standing round
Ling'rers alone on holy ground.—
Yon trees, as sullen as they seem,
Would tell too plain a tale I deem.
    Then say, when rock, and willow sweet,
White garland, yew, and cypress meet,
As here,—what should the group betoken?—
Speak, Lover!—though thy heart be broken!

———

ROMANZO *muffled in a cloak, solus.*

ROMANZO.   Hither they bend them slowly.   On
    this stone,
Green with the antique moss of many a year,
I think they mean to lay her ; and perform
The simple rites which country-people love
Around her gentle earth, ere it be borne
To consecrated grounds.   Young heralds twain
Have deckt the place already.—I 'll retire :
My presence might disturb the holy scene,
And I would be at peace as well as she !
My storm of life at length, I hope, is o'er ;
A stillness is upon me, like the pause
That ushers in eternity !—'Tis well !

                                [*Retires.*

The Procession enters.   Six Maidens strewing flowers.
    The Dirgers.   Then four Youths with a bier, on
    which SYLVIA *is laid beneath a virgin pall.*

AGATHA *supported by* STEPHANIA *and* ROSELLE.
GERONYMO, JACINTHA, *and Peasants following.*

DIRGE.

Wail ! wail ye o'er the dead !
  Wail ! wail ye o'er her !
Youth 's ta'en, and Beauty 's fled,
  O then deplore her !

Strew ! strew ye, Maidens ! strew
  Sweet flowers and fairest !
Pale rose, and pansy blue,
  Lily the rarest !
        Wail ! wail ye, &c.

Lay, lay her gently down
  On her moss pillow,
While we our foreheads crown
  With the sad willow !
        Wail ! wail ye, &c.

Raise, raise the song of wo,
  Youths, to her honour !
Fresh leaves, and blossoms throw,
  Virgins, upon her !
        Wail ! wail ye, &c.

Round, round the cypress bier
  Where she lies sleeping,
On every turf a tear,
  Let us go weeping !
        Wail ! wail ye, &c.

GERONYMO. Cease !—we must bear her on. 'T is
a long way to the village, and she must lie there a

time before the priest will give her *viaticum.*   Take
up the bier !

JACINTHA.   Should we leave the crown upon her
thus ?

Peasants.   Ay ! ay ! she was our May-Queen, and
shall go to the grave with all her honours about
her, like the greatest prince in Christendom.   Come
away !

Enter ANDREA.

ANDREA.   As I 'm a person, my old acquaintances !
Beauteous Mistress Stephania, your servant !   Lovely
Mistress Roselle, yours !   Ladies, one and all, I am
your most devoted—

Peasants.   The fiend ! the fiend !—Away !

[*They all run off, except* AGATHA.

AGATHA.   Come twenty fiends I 'll stay by thee,
my child !

ANDREA.   What a-vengeance do the people see in
me to frighten them ?—Alack !   I forgot that I was a
prodigy ! a *lusum naturum !*—Yet, after all, I do not
know that a pair of neatly-twisted antlers are such a
runaway matter ; unless I threatened to butt with
them !   Then as to cloven feet,—why, it is but having
four toes instead of ten, and make the most of it !
The 'longation of my ears, indeed, I consider as a
manifest improvement—an " accession " as we ele-
gantly term it.   So that, upon the whole, although
I should be loth to flatter myself, I think I am
a very personable-looking—*Tizzy*, Master Andrea !
tizzy voo ! look what is before you.   As I live, here
is a dead virgin !   It is she whom I am to elope with.
'Adad ! she 's a tender one !   I shall feel her no more,
than the flying horse *Packasses* (so they most asininely
call him) does a starved poet.   Now then for an act
of regeneration—   [*Approaching the bier.*

ROMANZO. [*Darting forward.*]
Miscreant, forbear! Hold off thy impious hands!
ANDREA. [*Falling on his knees.*]
O lud! the ghost of my unfortunate master!
ROMANZO. Slave, thou denied'st me! Ingrate!
Scorn of man!
Thou kneel'st for sacrifice at this pure altar,
And from the deep pollution of thy touch
Shalt cleanse it with thy blood!
AGATHA. [*Holding his arm.*]
Stay!—stay!—no blood—
Let there be none spill'd here. In death as life
Her bed be stainless!—O profane it not
With aught unsacred, or her cheek will grow
More pale with horror still!
ANDREA. 'S life! I must not let the old lady
lose the fruits of her eloquence! While she talks, I'll
walk: he may catch me if he can, but at least I will
show him a fair pair of heels for it— [*Runs away.*
AGATHA. O youth! dead Beauty's soldier!
pardon me!
The widow's, the unchilded mother's thanks,
Attend thee ever!—Let this act of thine
Make thy last pillow softer than the babe's
That smiling goes to Heaven!—O I have done ye
Most cruel wrong!
ROMANZO. Speak not of it, I pray you.
Let us stand here, on either side the shrine,
And weep in silence o'er her.

Enter FLORETTA.

Look! oh look!
Here is a little mourner come to join
Its sparkly tears with ours!

I

FLORETTA.   Where can my young beauty be
          That I have not found her?—
         Out, alas! this is not she
          With a shroud around her?

         Ay!—But stay! I scent a flower—
         Let me smell it—pah! pah!
         Well I know its deadly power—
          Come, unloose ye!—hah! hah!
            [*Takes off the magic wreath.*

Marble-one! Marble-one! rise from the tomb!
   Long hast thou slumber'd—Awake thee! awake
     thee!
Eyes, to your lustre! and cheeks, to your bloom!
   Lips, to your sweet smiling-office betake ye?

         Hark, she sighs! the Maiden sighs,
          Life and sense returning;
         Now she opes her pretty eyes
         Making a new morning!

         One white arm across her brow,
          Draws the sleepy fair one:
         Like a daystar rises now—
          Is she not a rare one?

         Still she sits in wonder so,
          With her shroud around her,
         Like a primrose in the snow,
          When the Spring has found her!

The Pride of the Valley, the Flower of the Glen,
Is breathing, and blooming, and smiling again!

          Kiss her, and press her,
          Caress her, and bless her,
    The sweet Maiden-Rose ! the Sun's Darling !
NEPHON. [*Above.*]
          Away ! come away !
OSME. [*Above.*]
          We have springes to lay,
    While thou'rt chattering here—
NEPHON. [*Above*].   Like a starling !
FLORETTA. Then fare thee well,
          My bonnibel !
    I would thou wert indeed a flower ;
          Thy breast should be
          My canopy,
    And I a queen in that sweet bower !
                              [*Vanishes.*

AGATHA. I did not hope such joy this side the
    grave :
O could my bosom clasp thee all—close ! close !
ROMANZO. This hand's enough for me.
    SYLVIA.   Dear Mother !—Friend !—
Anon I 'll say how much I love ye both :
I 'm faint as yet, and wandering ; lead me in.
                              [*Exeunt.*

    Enter NEPHON *with a suit like* ANDREA'S.

NEPHON. Now shall my disguise
          Cheat the spinster's eyes.
          And, as they shall rue,
          Cheat the demons' too.
          But I first must grow
          Some five feet or so,
          And swell out my span
          To the size of man.

[*Takes the shape of* ANDREA, *and assumes his dress.*
              Mortals, blame us not
                For the tricks we play ;
              Were ye fairies, what
                Would ye do, I pray ?
              I would lay a crumb,
                Could ye change your shapes,
              Ye would all become
                Mischievous as apes.
              Troth I think at present
                In the tricking trade,—
              Though not quite as pleasant,—
                Ye are just as bad !
[*Peasants without.*]   A miracle ! a miracle !
    NEPHON.   Here the boobies come,
                Pat as A, B, C.
              So behind the tomb
                I will nestle me.   [*Hides himself.*

                Enter the Peasants.

    All.   'T is true, 't is certain, 't is a fact to be
chronicled in tradition.   Here she lay ; here is her
crown.   She is alive again !   Let us go, and welcome
her back from darkness to daylight.   Huzza !
        [*As they go out,* NEPHON *twitches* ROSELLE *by
                                        the skirt.*
    NEPHON.   Mistress Roselle !   What, never a word
for your old friend and bottle-companion, Andrea ?
    ROSELLE.   Andrea !—I vow he is himself again !
Turn about :   let me see all your points, lest I be
jockeyed.   What have you done with your head-
gear ?   Have you been using the invaluable corn-
and-horn-rubber of little Beppo, the pedlar, that
you have gotten rid of your monstrosities ?

NEPHON.   Pooh ! 't was only a disguise to see if you had love enough to remember me.—Ah ! Mistress Roselle, you know by my eloquent eye in what a situation my heart is.

ROSELLE.   Why, as I guess, just under your left breast.

NEPHON.   No, gypsy ! but just under yours; there you have it, close prisoner, like a kernel in a filbert. —Hear me now : do you see this crown ?

ROSELLE.   Ay ; why do you untangle it ?

NEPHON.   It makes me mad to see that pale-faced simperer wear this beautiful chaplet, while my lovely Roselle deserves so much better to be May-Queen.

ROSELLE.   Why, as to that, indeed, I do not know for certain, but I think, as it were, that, mayhap, I shall look quite as well in it as my fine lady there.   But, if the plaguy thing won't fit me—

NEPHON.   Try it : I have taken out that twig, and if it does not fit you now, why cap never fitted a felon.   Only try it.

ROSELLE.   [*Putting it on.*]   By our ladykin, so it does !—O beautiful !—What do you think, friend Andrea ?   Am I a Venus in dimity, or not ?

NEPHON.   You are the most exquisite, incomparable, incomprehensible princess, that ever made her appearance in wooden clogs and stuff petticoats.— [*Aside.*]   Going !—going !—how she searches about for the pillow !

ROSELLE.   Stephania ! pull off my shoes—untie my sash—now ! now !—Where have you hidden the pillow ?—I 'm as sleepy to-night as a hedgehog.

NEPHON.   And shall lie as hard.   Hooh ! what pig-iron creatures these mortals are ! even the lightest

o' the species ! I should not like to be the miller,
your father, pretty maiden, if all my sacks were so
weighty.   [*Lays her upon the stone.*

Now, ye malicious couple ! spend your spite upon
this.   I have had a hint of your doings.

> Like a mist
>> kist
> By the matin ray,
> Or a shade
>> frayed,
> Thus I wane away.   [*Vanishes.*

Enter GRUMIEL *and* MOMIEL.

MOMIEL.   Ha ! here she lies.—Quick ! up with
        her, thou log !—
Let not the imp fry catch us.
    GRUMIEL.   Wasps !
    MOMIEL.   That blockhead !
He should have had no profit by success.
But, having served us, worn our livery still,
Which he so hated : now shall he assume
What will dislike him more,—a brutish tail,
The most ridiculous badge to smooth mankind.
Thus prosper they who covenant with the fiends !
                        [*Exeunt, bearing off* ROSELLE.

Scene IV.

Upon a lark's back, safe and soft,
Jaunty MORGANA sits aloft ;
And, while the sun-bird fans and sings,
Peeps through the lattice of his wings

At all beneath : Her light attendant,
OSME, floats like a starry pendant,
Beside the Queen ; to do her hest
Where'er her majesty thinks best.

MORGANA.   By this, I think, our host should be
  assembled.
Thou gav'st command to Nephon ?
  OSME.   Madam, I did.
  MORGANA.   Where he should place his guards,
  and line our bounds
Securely, did'st thou ?
  OSME.   Yes, so please Your Highness.
He would convene, too, on the level sward,
Minstrels and morris-dancers—
  MORGANA.   Foolish sprite !
We shall have other feats anon.   Two fiends
Already have transgressed my flowery verge,
And borne a sleeping shepherdess away.
Well, if no more : but, from your woods I deem
War, like a couchant lion, waits to spring
At opportunity.—Flit down, and know
What has been done : my breast is full of cares
Both for my kingdom and my shepherd twain.
  OSME.   A fairy Iris, I will make my bow
Of a bent sunbeam, and glide down as swift
As minnow doth the waterfall.   [*Vanishes.*
  MORGANA.   She lights !
And bird-like wings into the woody Vale,
Full of her errand.   It is featly done.—
Fall midway to the Earth, sweet Lark ! I pray.

The Scene closes.

Scene V.

Fair Lady, or sweet Sir, who look,
Perchance, into this wayward book,
Lay by your scenic eyes a moment ;
It is not for a raree-show meant.
I 've now some higher work to do
Than stipple graphic scenes for you.
Suffice to say, that smoother glade
Kept greener by a deeper shade,
Never by antler'd form was trod ;
Never was strown by that white crowd
Which nips with pettish haste the grass ;
Never was lain upon by lass
In harvest-time, when Love is tipsy
And steals to coverts like a gipsy
There to unmask his ruby face
In unreproved luxuriousness.
'T is true, in brief, of this sweet place,
What the tann'd Moon-bearer did feign
Of one rich spot in his own Spain :
The part just o'er it in the skies
Is the true seat of Paradise.*

Have you not oft, in the still wind,
Heard sylvan notes of a strange kind,
That rose one moment, and then fell
Swooning away like a far knell ?
Listen !—that wave of perfume broke
Into sea-music, as I spoke,
Fainter than that which seems to roar
On the moon's silver-sanded shore,
When through the silence of the night
Is heard the ebb and flow of light.

* The Arabians seem by this oriental assertion to have esti-
mated fully the value of their delicious moiety of Old Spain.

O shut the eye, and ope the ear !
Do you not hear, or think you hear,
A wide hush o'er the woodland pass
Like distant waving fields of grass ?—
Voices ?—ho ! ho !—a band is coming,
Loud as ten thousand bees a-humming,
Or ranks of little merry men
Tromboning deeply from the glen,
And now as if they changed, and rung
Their citterns small, and riband-slung,
Over their gallant shoulders hung !—
A chant ! a chant ! that swoons and swells
Like soft wind jangling meadow-bells ;
Now brave, as when in Flora's bower
Gay Zephyr blows a trumpet flower ;
Now thrilling fine, and sharp, and clear,
Like Dian's moonbeam dulcimer ;
But mixt with whoops, and infant laughter,
Shouts following one another after,
As on a hearty holyday
When Youth is flush, and full of May ;
Small shouts, indeed, as wild-bees knew
Both how to hum, and hollo too.
What ! is the living meadow sown
With dragon-teeth, as long agone ?
Or is an army on the plains
Of this sweet clime, to fight with cranes ?
Helmet and hauberk, pike and lance,
Gorget and glaive through the long grass glance ;
Red-men, and blue-men, and buff-men, small,
Loud-mouth'd captains, and ensigns tall,
Grenadiers, light-bobs, inch-people all,
They come ! They come ! with martial blore
Clearing a terrible path before ;

Ruffle the high-peak'd flags i' the wind,
Mourn the long-answering trumpets behind,
Telling how deep the close files are—
Make way for the stalwart sons of war !
Hurrah ! the buff-cheek'd bugle band,
Each with a loud reed in his hand !
Hurrah ! the pattering company,
Each with a drum-bell at his knee !
Hurrah ! the sash-capt cymbal swingers !
Hurrah ! the klingle-klangle ringers !
Hurrah ! hurrah ! the elf-knights enter,
Each with his grasshopper at a canter ?
His tough spear of a wild oat made,
His good sword of a grassy blade,
His buckram suit of shining laurel,
His shield of bark, emboss'd with coral !
See how the plumy champion keeps
His proud steed clambering on his hips,
With foaming jaw pinn'd to his breast,
Blood-rolling eyes, and arched crest !
Over his and his rider's head
A broad-sheet butterfly banner spread,
Swoops round the staff in varying form,
Flouts the soft breeze, but courts the storm.
    Hard on the prancing heels of these
Come on the pigmy Thyades !
Mimics, and mummers, masqueraders,
Soft flutists, and sweet serenaders,
Guitarring o'er the level green,
Or tapping the parch'd tambourine,
As swaying to, and swaying fro,
Over the stooping flowers they go,
That laugh within their greeny breasts
To feel such light feet on their crests,

And ev'n themselves a-dancing seem
Under the weight that presses them.

    But hark ! the trumpet's royal clangour
Strikes silence with a voice of anger :
Raising its broad mouth to the sun
As he would bring Apollo down,
The in-back'd, swoln, elf-winder fills
With its great roar the fairy hills ;
Each woodland tuft for terror shakes,
The field-mouse in her mansion quakes,
The heart-struck wren falls through the branches,
Wide stares the earwig on his haunches ;
From trees which mortals take for flowers,
Leaves of all hues fall off in showers ;
So strong the blast, the voice so dread,
'T would wake the very fairy dead !

    Disparted now, half to each side,
Athwart the curled moss they glide,
Then wheel and front, to edge the scene,
Leaving a spacious glade between ;
With small round eyes that twinkle bright
As moon-tears on the grass of night,
They stand spectorial, anxious all,
Like guests ranged down a dancing hall.
Some graceful pair, or more, to see
Winding along in melody.

    Nor pine their little orbs in vain,
For borne in with an oaten strain
Three petty Graces, arm-entwined,
Reel in the light curls of the wind ;
Their flimsy pinions sprouted high
Lift them half-dancing as they fly ;
Like a bright wheel spun on its side
The rapt three round their centre slide,

And as their circling has no end
Voice into sister voice they blend,
Weaving a labyrinthian song
Wild as the rings they trace along,
A dizzy, tipsy roundelay, —
Which I am not to sing, but they.

TRIO.

We the Sun's bright daughters be !
  As our golden wings may show ;
Every land, and every sea,
  Echoes our sweet ho-ran ho !
      Round, and round, and round we go
      Singing our sweet ho-ran ho !

Over heath, and over hill,
  Ho-ran, hi-ran, ho-ran ho !
At the wind's unruly will,
  Round, and round, and round we go.

Through the desert valley green,
  Ho-ran, hi-ran, ho-ran ho !
Lonely mountain-cliffs between,
  Round, and round, and round we go.

Into cave, and into wood,
  Ho-ran, hi-ran, ho-ran ho !
Light as bubbles down the flood,
  Round, and round, and round we go.

By the many tassell'd bowers,
  Ho-ran, hi-ran, ho-ran ho !
Nimming precious bosom flowers,
  Round, and round, and round we go.

Dimpling o 'er the grassy meads,
    Ho-ran, hi-ran, ho-ran ho !
Shaking gems from jewell'd heads,
    Round, and round, and round we go.

After bee, and after gnat,
    Ho-ran, hi-ran, ho-ran ho !
Hunting bird, and chasing bat,
    Round, and round, and round we go.

Unto North, and unto South,
    Ho-ran, hi-ran, ho-ran ho !
In a trice to visit both,
    Round, and round, and round we go.

To the East, and to the West
    Ho-ran, hi-ran, ho-ran ho !
To the place that we love best,
    Round, and round, and round we go.

First Elve.	Sweet ! sweet !
Second Elve.	O how finely.
	They do spark their feet !
Third Elve.	Divinely !
	I can scarcely keep from dancing,
	'T is so wild a measure !
Fourth Elve.	E'en the heavy steeds are prancing
	With uneasy pleasure !
Second Elve.	Smooth the cadence of the music,
	Smooth as wind !
Fifth Elve.	O me !—I 'm dew-sick !—
All.	Glutton ! glutton ! you 've been drinking.
	Till your very eyes are winking !
Fourth Elve.	Put him to bed in that green tuft.
Second Elve.	He should not have a bed so soft !

First Elve.   Let him be toss'd into a thistle !

Third Elve.   We'll tease his nose with barley-
bristle !

Sixth Elve.   Or paint his face with that ceruse
Which our fine bella-donnas use,
The sweet conserve of maiden-
blushes.

First Elve.   Or cage him in a crib of rushes ;
There let him lie in verdant jail
Till he out-mourns the nightingale.

Fourth Elve.   Sad thing ! what shall become of
thee,
When thy light nature wanes to something new ?
Say'st thou, sad thing ?—

Fifth Elve.   O let me, let me be
A gliding minnow in a stream of dew !

Second Elve.   The sot !

First Elve.   The dolt.

Sixth Elve.   The epicure !
'Twere wrong to call him else, I'm
sure.

Each twilight-come,
At beetle-drum,
For nectar he a-hunting goes,
The twisted bine
He stoops for wine,
Or sups it fresh from off the rose.

In violet blue
He pokes for dew,
And gapes at Heaven for starry tears ;
Till Phœbus laughs,
He crows and quaffs,
Frighting the lark with bacchant cheers.

From night to morn
His amber horn
He fills at every honey-fountain,
And draineth up
Each flowery cup
That brims with balm on mead or mountain.

Second Elve.   Hi ! hi !

Fourth Elve.   Whither ? whither ?

Second Elve.   I must try
To get that feather
Floating near the stilly sun.

Fourth Elve.   Now you have it, clap it on !
What a gallant bonnet-plume,
Ruby-black with golden bloom !

Second Elve.   It must have belonged, I swear,
To some gaudy bird of air ;
One of the purple-crested team
who fly
With the Junonian curricle ;
Or he that with rich breast, and
tawny eye,
Flames at the Sminthian
chariot-wheel.

First Elve.   But where is Nephon ? who can
tell ?

Seventh Elve.   How wondrous grand he 's grown
of late !

Eighth Elve.   And walks so high ! and slaps his
pate
Ten times a moment, as the state
Of Fairyland depended on him,
Or tit-mice had agreed to crown
him.

Third Elve.   And takes such mighty airs upon
                him
                As I can witness : 'T was but now
                I challenged him to ride the bough,
                When pursing bigly—" Silly thou !
                Trouble me not " said he, and
                    stalk'd
                As stiff as if a radish walk'd
                Past me, forsooth !

First Elve.   He has not talk'd
                Of any body but himself
                This mortal day.

Second Elve. Conceited elf !
                Would he were bottled on a
                    shelf !

Osme.   Fay-ladies be not scandalous,
                Ah, speak not of poor Nephon thus !

Third Elve.   Then wherefore should he sneer
                    at us ?

Seventh Elve. He grows more haughty every day
                'Cause he 's the queen's factotal fay,
                And scorns with other elves to play.

Fourth Elve. When will his Excellence appear ?

Osme.   He sent a wild-dove messenger
                To bid us all assemble here,
                On the green glade ; for he had
                    some
                Great work in hand.—

Seventh Elve. The saucy gnome !
                " Bid us," forsooth !

Floretta.   I wish he 'd come !
                I hear on distant heaths behind
                A hare-bell weeping to the wind,
                Unkind Floretta ! ah, unkind,
                To leave me thus forsaken !

OSME.   I
                Will mount a crowback to the sky,
                Morgana waits for me on high.
                [*Laughter without.*]
All.   Hist ! hist !
[*Without.*]   Ha ! ha ! ha !
All.   List ! list !
[*Without.*]   Ha ! ha ! ha !
All.   In the noisy name of thunder
                What is all this rout, I wonder ?
[*Without.*]   Ha ! ha ! ha ! ha ! ha !

Enter NEPHON *with his lap full of flowers.*

NEPHON.   Lady and gentlemen fays, come buy !
No pedlar has such a rich packet as I.

    Who wants a gown
        Of purple fold,
    Embroidered down
        The seams with gold ?
            See here !—a Tulip richly laced
            To please a royal fairy's taste !

    Who wants a cap
        Of crimson grand ?
    By great good hap
        I 've one on hand :
            Look, sir !—a Cock's-comb, flowering red,
            'T is just the thing, sir, for your head !

    Who wants a frock
        Of vestal hue ?
    Or snowy smock ?—
        Fair maid, do you ?
            O me !—a Ladysmock so white !
            Your bosom's self is not more bright !

                    K

Who wants to sport
    A slender limb ?
I 've every sort
    Of hose for him :
        Both scarlet, striped, and yellow ones :
        This Woodbine makes such pantaloons !

Who wants—(hush ! hush !)
    A box of paint ?
'T will give a blush,
    Yet leave no taint :
        This Rose with natural rouge is fill'd,
        From its own dewy leaves distill'd.

Then lady and gentlemen fays, come buy !
You never will meet such a merchant as I.

[*A sprig of broom falls at his feet.*]

NEPHON.   Bow ! wow !
FLORETTA.   What is this,
    With spikes and thorns, but not a leaf on ?
NEPHON.   By my fay ! I think it is
    A rod for Nephon.
    Whe-e-e-w !
    I shall be whipt, as sure as I
    Stand here—Holla ! you idle Elves !
    Leap, skip, hop, jump, bounce, fly,
    And range yourselves,
    Obedient, till I lesson you
    In what you have, each one, to do.
    You, sir ! you, sir ! you, sir ! you !
        Knight, and squire, and stout soldado,
    To your charge, good men and true,
        We commit this happy meadow,

From yon dingle to that dell,
  See no hostile foot profane it ;
And let minute-trumpets tell
  How ye steadily maintain it.
Drums strike up, and clarions bray !
  Ranks i' the rear take open order !
Left foot foremost ! March away !
  On by the Valley 's midland border !
           [*Exit, with the rest of the army.*

ACT V.

Scene I.

NCONSCIOUS ANDREA once more
Passes the shadowy border o'er ;
For though each opening glade, along
The wild, war-blasted marches, throng
With slow-paced elfin sentinels,
Wo be to him who makes or mells,
By word or deed, with man's condition
But in the way of his commission !
Ev'n to be heard or seen at all
Is held a crime most capital ;
And therefore comes it that so few
Spirits have met our mortal view,
Although such things, beyond a doubt,
Exist, if we could find them out.

ANDREA. 'T is with me, only out of the frying-
pan into the fire : I live the life of a flying-fish : no
sooner do I 'scape this shark than that cormorant
pounces upon me ; when I dive for safety from the
beak of the air-devil, I find the jaws of the water-
devil most hospitably open to receive me.—Saint
Bridget be my protector ! here come my old friends,
the Moorish ambassadors !—just in the nick of time
to give my speech a new proof and illustration !—

Again, I say, miserable! thrice miserable Ribobolo!
—It is not two skips of the sun since thou wert on the
point of being cut down like a flower of the field, in
all the pride of thy beauty, and now, to crown thy ill-
fortune, here are two devils come to possess thee.—
Save ye, gentlemen!

Enter GRUMIEL *and* MOMIEL *with* ROSELLE.

MOMIEL. Ha! ha! thou scape-goat!—art thou
    caught again?
Stir not a pace, but tremble where thou stand'st.

ANDREA. With all my might, sir!—I shake where
I grow, as if I were about to turn into an aspen.

MOMIEL. See! we have done thy duty, thou
    forsworn,
Contemptible wretch! This is the maiden-prize
Thou should'st have brought us, and been man again.

ANDREA. Lud-amercy! here is one of my mountain landladies! Mistress Roselle, as I'm a person,
the miller's daughter!

MOMIEL. This?

ANDREA. This! Ay this! I'll stake my ears
on 't!—Odso! Now that I call the matter to mind,
Satan was guilty of her abduction : he gathered her
and her sister as they were growing, posy-fashion,
beside the mill-pond, to sweeten the air of his roaring
kitchen. Where is t'other pullet? has he spitted her
already?

GRUMIEL. Ha! ba! ha! ha! here was a strata-
    gem!

MOMIEL. Curse thee, vile oaf! Dost laugh at
    me? I'll tear thee!

GRUMIEL. Come on? I'll writhe about thee as a
    snake,
And twist thy bones like gristle—

MOMIEL.   Help ! help, king !

ANDREA.   Well done, my chickens !   To 't, boys !
Excellent !   Five to one upon Spitfire !—At him,
Snap-dragon !—To 't !—Bravo !—Now if they would
only eat each other up, after the precedent of the two
cats in the saw-pit, ' twould be a *desideratum* much to
desired.—Hilloah ! are heaven, earth, and purgatory
coming together ?

ARARACH *descends amid thunder and lightning.*
Attendant Fiends.

ARARACH.   Bunglers again !—Hurry them to the
    flames
As I commanded : Sweep them from my sight,
Rebels ! that serve their passions and not mine !

    [*Exeunt fiends with* GRUMIEL *and* MOMIEL.
Myself, I find, though sore against my will,
Both chief and actor must be in their business.
Come hither, clown !—Take thy man-shape again,
See what thou ow'st my pity.   Get thee gone !
There is thy road ; 't will lead thee to thy friends,
Whom thou may'st hither fetch, if they will come,
To bear this maiden grave-ward.   We 'll depart !
See that yon corse burden not long our realm,
Or thou, and all thy rout, shall lie as cold !

                                [*Ascends.*

ANDREA.   My stars ! what a—phew ! he has left
after him : like the last sighs of ten thousand expiring
candles.   It is enough to smother all the hives in
Sicily.   Now if he would be only satisfied to live
like a man of reputation, he might earn an honest
livelihood by travelling as a sulphur-merchant to the
North (where, I am told, there is a great demand for
that article), or by selling matches through the streets,

-two bundles for a half-penny. But ods bobs ! why
ꜱ I stand here lecturing on commercial affairs when
don't know but his pestiferous majesty may descend
another cloud of such frankincense, and I shall be
noked to the flavour of Westphalia bacon ? Well,
it were only from one feature in my face, videlicet,
y tongue, I would even swear that I was the identi-
ıl son of my mother !—Fly, Andrea, as fast as thy
gs can carry thee !   [*Exit.*

ARARACH *descends again.*

ARARACH.   Now let me use my skill. Thou sleep-
        ing earth,
ake thou the form of Sylvia, the May-Queen !
ınd lie there in that thicket, till one comes
√hom I would lime for a decoy, to bring
he bird I love about her.   So !—'tis done !—
                                    [*Ascends again.*

The Scene closes.

Scene II.

Peasants, in simple conclave met,
Are round the wake-stone gravely set,
Perplext to guess what chance befell
Their lost companion, young Roselle.

STEPHANIA.   O sister ! sister ! what has become
f you ?—I will never go home without you, if I were
ꜱ seek a thousand years !—What should I say to my
ιother when she asked for her pretty Rose ?

GERONYMO.   Nay, weep not so heartily, I pray
you : be not in such woful contrition.   The case is
not so bad, by a hundred miles, as you think it : for,
look you now, it stands thus, or in other words,
here 't is : You have lost your sister beyond recovery;
good—

STEPHANIA.   Begone, fickle-hearted turncoat !—
If I could even forget your treachery, I am not in the
mood now to hear such a prig discoursing.

GERONYMO.   Why, very well, there 't is : I am a
prig.   Bear witness to that : she calls me—prig, and
refuses to hear condolement.

First Peasant.   Go to ! you are ejected, and may
wear the willow.

GERONYMO.   No matter ! 't is all very well ! very
well indeed !—I will hang myself some of these fine
mornings, and then, mayhap, she will see what it
is to wound the heart of a sensible-plant like me, by
calling him a prig and turncoat.   Cruel Mrs Stephania ! I thought your soul was as tender as a chicken,
but now I find it is harder than Adam's aunt or
marble !

STEPHANIA.   If you wish to soften it again, you
will find out my sister.   I can think of nothing else
till she be discovered.

GERONYMO.   Say no more, but put your trust
in my zigacity.   Above ground and beneath sky,
I 'll ferret her out, though she were hid in a blind
nutshell.

Second Peasant.   So, friend ! whither are you going?

Enter ANDREA.

ANDREA.   Indeed I cannot particularly say : but
going I am !—I have taken up the trade of a water-
wheel lately, and am always going ! moreover betoken

that, like it, I cannot get out of the pickle in which the malice of my enemies has placed me, but am continually soused over head and ears by a flood of misfortune. However, time cures all sorrows, and philosophy, the remainder.—Saw you any peasants about here? clowns, clodpoles, *popolaccio*, dregs, that is to say, honest, foolish kind of persons?

Peasants. Why, I hope we be such: what else do you take us for?

ANDREA. By this light, now that I observe it, so ye are. Ye answer the description exactly: no hue-and-cry ever gave the dimensions of a banditti more precisely. Well; and wherefore in the dumps, my honest, foolish kind of neighbours?

GERONYMO. Why if it so please you, here 't is now—

ANDREA. This is a logicizer: you may always know a logicizer, by his laying down the law with his forefinger. Save thy invisible bellows, thou oracular fellow; I know all thou wouldst say, better than if there was a glass window in thy stomach. Ye are seeking for one of your lost lambs, my pastors?

Peasants. By the mass, so we are! He must be a witch, neighbours, to tell us this without knowing it.

ANDREA. Follow your noses, and I will undertake to lead you by them to where she is: I owe her as much gratitude as would fill a wine-flagon, pie-dish, brandy-flask, et cetera, nappercyhand, nappercyhand. She and her sister made a cramm'd fowl of me, I thank them. Indeed, if a stone could melt, I had poured out my heart at her feet, in expression of love and affliction. But this is irreverent! Come along: 't is not five-score yards beyond the bowsprits I have promised to tow ye by.

Peasants. Willingly, and thank you.   [*Exeunt.*

Scene changes to another part of the Glen.

Enter ANDREA *and the Peasants.*

ANDREA.   There ! in that thicket, that bramble-bush; if your eyes be not scratched out by leaping into it, you will see her there.

Peasants.   Well, come with us, and show it more catacullycully.

ANDREA.   Ay, to be sure I will !—Go on ; I 'll be whipper-in of your whole pack.   Proceed, I tell ye ! it is all before you, as a pedlar carries his knapsack.

Peasants.   Lead away, then !

ANDREA.   Right ; you are in the very track of it : I shall cry out "roast-beef !" when you are about to tumble upon her.

Peasants.   Good !   Proceed, Geronymo.   Our guide will come after us.

ANDREA.   O, doleful ! woful ! racks ! torments ! thumbscrews !—O my great toe ! my great toe !

Peasants.   What is the matter?

ANDREA.   My great toe, I say !—O, now are the sins of my ancestors coming against me !—The gout ! the gout !—I cannot stir an inch farther, if I got the bribe of a secretary !—Go on, go on : if you stay here making mouths at my foot it will only grow the more angry.

Peasants.   Well, remain here for us, while we search the bushes.

ANDREA.   Speed ye; neighbours !—Hark'ee !

Peasants.   What ?

ANDREA.   Ye will be here when ye come back, eh ?

Peasants.   Ay, certainly.

ANDREA.   Why then, meantime, I will put my foot in a sling, and prepare to hop off with ye.   Good-

bye !—Oo ! such a twinge ! as if the fiend's claw and
my foot struck a bargain for ever ! Oo !

Peasants. On, folks ! on !—He must be sorely
afflicted to make such a piteous howling, and such
heinously ill-favoured grimaces. How he lolls his
tongue out at us, like a mad dog ! We are well rid of
him. [*Exeunt.*

ANDREA. 'Slife ! why was I not a politician ? a
Machiavelian ?—I would overreach his Spanish majesty himself, who, they tell me, is the very flower of
dissimulation, the pink of hypocrisy.—Those empty-
pates ! those human ostriches ! that run their heads
into a bush and think themselves hidden from danger,
because it is hidden from them !—I know more of
jurisprudence than to play at blind man's buff with
Mephistopheles and his convent of Black Friars.
Well, he may enlist them all under his pitchy ensign,
but he shall not have me for a fugueman, I will
rather be a fugitive ! . *Exit.*

Scene III.

Tell one, young Prophetess ! that now
Lean'st o'er my arm, thine anxious brow,
The while my cheek delighted feels
Thy rolling curls, like little wheels
Course up and down that swarthy plain,—
Tell me, young Seer ! I say again,
What does my flying pencil trace
To tinge with doubtful bloom thy face ?
Why should thy breast suspicious heave ?
What doth thy glistening eye perceive ?
Can thy shrewd innocence divine
The mystery of this sketch of mine ?

Two graceful forms beneath a shade
Through its green drapery half survey'd :
An arm stolen round a slender waist,
Lips to a white hand gently prest ;
A manly brow that wants not much
An alabaster one to touch,
'Neath it pure-flushing ; in repose
Laid, almost like a fainting rose,
That turns her with a secret sigh
To some boy Zephyr whispering nigh,
And in his airy breast doth seek
To hide her deeply blushing cheek,
Or, lest she swoon, reclineth there
Her red cheek on his scented hair.

Half-smiling Maiden ! whose pink breast
Peeps like the ruddock's o'er its nest,
Or moss-bud from its peaked vest,
What to thy simple thinking is
Th' interpretation of all this?
I 'll tell thee, if thou say'st amiss :
A youthful pair, met in a grove,
Arm-intertwined : What should this prove ?—
Maiden. "I think it must be—Love ! "

ROMANZO *and* SYLVIA.

ROMANZO.   After the Night how lovely springs
    the Morn !
After the shower how freshly blooms the green !
After the clouds and tempest of our fate,
How sweetly breaks the beauty of the sky,
And hangs its rainbow ev'n amid our tears !—
Now Mercy joins us in her circling arms,

And, like a beauteous mother, wishes us
All joy that can betide !—Is not her blessing
Already come upon us ?   Is not this
Perfect beatitude ?

    SYLVIA.   O, but I fear
It will not last for ever !—'T is too sweet.

    ROMANZO.   What should Heaven find in either of
        us two
That should provoke its shaft ?—No ! we will live,
Bosom to bosom thus, like harmless doves,
And so be spared for our great innocence !—
Look up and smile !

    SYLVIA.   Nay, I am of thy mind—
Ecstasy is too deeply-soul'd to smile.
I am more near to weep ; but such fond tears
As flow'rets, ill-intreated of the night,
Shed, when the morn-winds sing i' the Eastern gate
That father Sun doth rise.

    ROMANZO.   Is not this love
A happy thing ? a fountain of new life,
Another win of blood within the heart
That floods the ebbing veins ; and teems new life
Through all those ruby channels ?—Oh, it is
Warmest of bosom-friends !—Joy'st not to feel
This downy bird rustle within thy arms,
Choosing his fragrant bed ; as fond as he,
The nectar-bibbing fly, who doth disturb,
With most uxorious care, yon rose, the while
He settles in her breast ?

    SYLVIA.   Is Love a bird ?

    ROMANZO.   A boy !—with curls of crisped gold,
        like thine :
Lips like the fresh sea coral : in his cheek
The sleepless Laughter cradles ; and above

Perpetual Sport rides in his humorous eye.
This guest of man hath to his use beside
A quiver, and light arrows, and a bow ;
With which he stings his votaries' willing hearts,
Aiming from beauty's hills, or vantage-ground,
Where he can light : then flies (for pinions he
Fleéces the wand'ring gossamer) to tend
The wounds his bolt hath made ; and often there,
Like a good surgeon, pillows till they heal,
Or sweetly cruel makes them bleed again.
This is Love's picture ; and his page of life
Writ in Time's chronicle.

    SYLVIA.   Sure it must be
A marvellous child !

    ROMANZA.   O, 't is a winsome boy !
And tells such pleasant tales, and sings such songs,
With harp gay-tinkling like a Troubadour,
That icy nuns through charitable grates
Thrust forth their lovely arms to pamper him ;
And so he often wounds them, while they leave
Their bosoms undefended.

    SYLVIA.   I would hear
Some of his minstrelsy.

    ROMANZO.   Why so thou hast :
He speaks through various lips ; even now through
    mine.

    SYLVIA. Ah ! thou deceiv'st me : thou art he !
    but clothed
In shape more godlike.

    ROMANZO.   No ! his deputy,
Teaching thee his pure doctrine, and sweet truths,
How wilt thou e'er repay me ? O, will all
Thy heart be half enough, for making thee
So wise a scholar in this book of joy?

I've taught thee Love's sweet lesson o'er,
A task that is not learn'd with tears :
  Was Sylvia e'er so blest before
In her wild, solitary years ?
     Then what does he deserve, the Youth,
     Who made her con so dear a truth !

  Till now in silent vales to roam,
Singing vain songs to heedless flowers,
  Or watch the dashing billows foam,
Amid thy lonely myrtle bowers,
     To weave light crowns of various hue,—
     Were all the joys thy bosom knew.

  The wild bird, though most musical,
Could not to thy sweet plaint reply ;
  The streamlet, and the waterfall,
Could only weep when thou did'st sigh !
     Thou could'st not change one dulcet word
     Either with billow, or with bird.

  For leaves, and flowers, but these alone,.
Winds have a soft discoursing way ;
  Heav'n's starry talk is all its own,—
It dies in thunder far away.
     E'en when thou would'st the Moon beguile
     To speak,—she only deigns to smile !

  Now, birds and winds, be churlish still,
Ye waters keep your sullen roar,
  Stars be as distant as ye will,—
Sylvia need court ye now no more :
     In Love there is society
     She never yet could find with ye !

" Then what does he deserve, the Youth ? "—
Might he but touch that moist and rubious lip,
Ev'n Dian could not frown !—the wind-kist rose
Is not less pure because she's bountiful
When Zephyr wooes her chastely.   Be thou, then,
Who art as fair, as kind !—   [*Kisses her.*
                              O !—O ! a kiss !
Sweeter than May-dew to the thirsty flower,
Or to Jove's half-clung bird, his clamorous food
From minist'ring Hebe's hand !—

SYLVIA.   Would it were sweeter,
For thy sake, than it is !—We are betroth'd,
And so I hold my petty treasures thine,
My lord and husband.

ROMANZO.   Therefore in their use
I will be frugal, since thou 'rt generous.—

SYLVIA.   Hark ! hark ! a cry !—

ROMANZO.   Fear not !—thou 'rt in my arms.

ANDREA *without.*

Alas ! alas !—Help ! help !—Do I live amongst
Saracens or Turkies ?—No pity ? no assistance !—
The good dame ! the excellent old lady ! Kidnapt !
transposed ! elevated !—She who saved me from that
mad-pated fellow my master !

SYLVIA.   My mother !

ROMANZO.   What 's this ruffian hurly?   Speak !

Enter ANDREA.

Help, I say ! — Rescue ! rescue ! — If ye have
hearts the size of queen-cakes, let your swords
leap from your scabbards, and cut down these
sans-culottes ! these Carbonari ! sons of the Black
Prince ! whelps of Belzebub !—O master ! Master !
turn away the eyes of your wrath from me upon those

dingy freebooters !—Lamentable ! O lamentable ! lamentable !

ROMANZO. Speak ! Who ?—who ?—

SYLVIA. If thou hast pity, speak !

ANDREA. Pity !—Am I not weeping my eyes out ?—What can I do more ?—Are either of ye half as pitiful a fellow ?—Do I stand nonchanically here like a statue, as if I were gasping for bob-cherries, or had set my mouth for a fly-trap ?—Pity, indeed !— Am I not shouting, ranting, and calling down vengeance upon the heads of these nefarious women-stealers as fast as tiles in a storm ? What call you this but pity ?—active, stirring, practical, — I say, practical pity ?—Oons ! I should have been president of some humane society, or an overseer of the poor at the least, had I remained turnspit to the Sardinian ambassador in England.

SYLVIA. Agony chokes me !—O I shall go mad !

ROMANZO. Dastardly hound ! I'll shake thy story out of thee !

ANDREA. Pray do not ; it would discompose me much in the telling of it, I assure you. Mark me now—" Here 't is ! " as neighbour Geronymo says ; or thus it stands, or this is the tot of the matter. We proceeded on our excursion, or incursion (to speak critically, for we were about to enter the preserve of a Nabob, though, indeed, we had a special licence from his diabolical lordship)—Well !—Take your knuckles off my throat, I beseech you, sir ; my words come out *pip ! pip !* like bullets from a popgun. Well—as I was saying—the peasants and I, or, in other words, I and the peasants, which you will,—proceeded on our progress to seek for young Mrs Roselle, the miller's

L

daughter, in the wood, just there, over your worship's nose, where the grass is so thin, it would hardly fodder a goose. Well ! so far, so good—A little more vent, if you please, sir ! I shall never run out else. Well !—When we had come thither, lo and behold ye ! no Mrs Roselle ; not the print of her shoe upon the moss, though she wore beechen ones an inch thick, and clouted from heel to toe with six-penny hobnails. Well !—no maid o' the mill, as I told ye, was to be found there, but in her stead the shapes and figures of one Mrs Sylvia, as the peasants entitled her : some country-hoyden, I surmise, that purls a little through an oaten-pipe, and infests these parts in a sheep-keeping character,—a "dear Pastora," as one might say, a Mrs Simplicity—O ! your worship ! do not tuck that thumb so inexorably under my gizzard as if you were nailing up wall-fruit—You 'll spoil my story !

ROMANZO.   Would I could strangle thee, and hear thee after !

ANDREA.   Why, indeed, hanging is almost too good a death for an informer ; but it is considered more politic to reward him. However, to proceed as we went on : I being foremost, that is foremost in the rear, I *debouche* towards dame Agatha, who, indeed, was coming by hasty marches to warn us of some danger, and I communicate to her my intelligence—

ROMANZO.   Well ? — What did she ? — what ?— what ?—speak it

ANDREA.   Fell all of a heap like a haycock, your worship ; and thereupon darted immediately into the wood as if her heels were loaded with quicksilver ; from thence bolted into the arms of a couple of Black

Hussars, who carried her off to perdition. And so, if they don't live happy, I hope—

SVLVIA. Fly, fly, and save her !—O your mercy Heavens. [*Swoons.*

ROMANZO. Hear me, thou villain !—On thy hopes of life,
Here and hereafter, guard this lovely one,
Sustain, restore, and tend her, while hard fate
Keeps me from that dear office,—or as sure
As lightning blasts, thy doom is fixt. [*Exit.*

ANDREA. Indeed, so it appears : to be ever surrounded and o'erwhelmed by innumerable and indescribable miseries and mischances, accidents and offences, dreadful calamities and singular occurrences ! —They come as thick upon me as if they were showered from a dredging-box ! I am powdered with sorrows and afflictions ! Salted, peppered, pickled ! roasted, baisted, stewed, fried, crimped, scarified, tossed like a pancake, and beaten like a batter, upon all occasions ! Finally, I have been cooked up into a devil, and may perhaps be buried alive in a minced-pie to be served up at a Christmas-feast among the Cannibals. Nevertheless, I will endeavour to revive this lovely maiden according to the prescriptions of Galen and Hippocrypha—

[*Raises* SYLVIA *in his arms.*

Truly, my adventures follow one another with marvellous dexterity : if they were only printed I might string them together like ballads, and sell them by the yard as they do popular songs, or Bologna sausages : I should have every mob-cap in the neighbourhood peeping out of the attics, and have copper jingling about me as if I were playing the triangle,— could I only bring myself to chant my own deeds for

remuneration.—Here now am I, without ever having
studied more of the Healing Art than a farrier's dog,
—here am I installed as physician-general of this
uninhabited district, and condemned under the
penalty of bastinado and carbonization, to raise this
mortal from the dead, as if I had invented an universal
restorative !—'Sbodikins ! it is too much ! were my
shoulders as broad as Mount Hatless, I could not
long bear this load of negotiations that is laid upon
them ! — If I were anything less than the most
tender-hearted Samaritan in all Christendom, I would
leave this pretty faint-away here to get well as she
could, by the study of "Every man his own physi-
cian," and take to my heels like a dancing bear when
I am threatened with such a flagellation.   But no
matter !—the heart of man was made for misfortune
as an ass's back for a packsaddle.   We must all be
stocks and philosophers !—I 'll run for a capful of the
limpid to baptize her.   [*Exit.*

Scene closes.

Scene IV.

Slowly as Twilight lifts her veil
To show her wintry forehead pale,
Unto the frore Antarctic world,
A lurid curtain is upfurled,
Disclosing the huge pedestals
That prop the necromantic walls ;
But still so heavily it looms,
Clouds under clouds with volumy wombs,
That scarce it seems indeed to rise,
Too ponderous for the fleecy skies.
At length, by inch and inch appear,

The portals of the Sorcerer ;
And yawning like a charnel-gate
Ope to admit a corse of state,
The bossy valves scream as they swing
On brazen hinge, scarce opening
Their slothful jaws for their own king.

Enter ARARACH *and Fiends with* ROMANZO
prisoner.

ARARACH.   Enter before us !—
I will not have him torn with thongs, nor pierced
With barbed instruments ; nor pincht, nor crampt ;
These are but laughing pains to such wild tortures
As I 'll afflict him with : he shall not bellow
His furnace pains shut in an ox of brass,
Like him whose craft was proved upon himself ;
Nor shall his lopt or lengthen'd form be stretch'd
On iron bed, accommodately fill'd
By every guest, pygmy, or stout, or tall.
Trite code of agonies ! that writhe the frame,
But hardly wring the mind.   Peasants who have
Their feelings in their flesh, and none more inward,
Shrink at the bloody pincers : but high natures
Who feel not in their clay, despise all pangs
That reach no deeper.—I will plague him there !
In a refined, imaginative way ;
And work upon his sensibility,
Not on his senses, which he 'd reck as much
As the wild Indian at the stake, or he
Who burnt his hand for bravery.—What ho !
Is the stage rear'd ?
Fiend.   Dismiel, the machinist,
Is hard about it, lord : you hear the clang,

And music of his anvil, which doth sing
At every stroke, like a cathedral bell,
And every iron tingles in the hand
Of his accomplices.

   ARARACH.   Go ! quicken him
With a few stings i' the elbow.—And thou, too,
See if my quaint device go smoothly off,
Ere the Phantasma pass before his eyes,
Whom we would entertain with feats and shows
As such a guest deserves. If one particular
Fail in the presentation, even by chance,
I 'll hold thee punishable : Mark it well !

                   [*Exit. The Fiends vanish.*

Scene V.

A winding walk of moss, between
Two hedge-rows of sweet aubepine,
With English White-thorn, much the same
Both shrub and its Provencal name.
Yet still I think our homely word
Is much,—ay much !—to be preferr'd,—
Except it more convenient be
In rhyme, as it was now to me.
I love this racy northern Land,
And think its tongue both sweet and grand,
Though mongrel authors may abuse it,
Because they know not how to use it.
Green Albion, shake him from thy breast,
The renegade ! who thinks not best
Both thee, and thine, of all the sun
Looks with his golden eye upon !
As she who gave us human birth

Is dear,—why not our parent-earth?
Shallow pronouncers may call this
Poorness of soul, and prejudice;
Why then, 't is weak to love our mothers
Better, one whit, than those of others!
If this philosophy be sound,
By no one tie is nature bound;
We have free warrant to disclaim
All laws of kindred, blood, and name,
Like Spanish kings, despite of taunts,
Marry our nieces or our aunts,
And by the same licentious rule
Tell our grave father he 's a fool,
Scoundrel, or liar,—call him out,
Or cuff him in a fistic bout,
Owing no more in such a case
Than bankers do to Henry Hase;
All home-affections are absurd,
And duty is an old-wife's word:
Who feels a brave indifference
For natural bond, or natural sense,
Is, in our modern Teucer's sight,
The only true Cosmopolite!

No more! no more!—I neither can,
Nor would I, write—"Essays on Man;"
Here are some Maidens to assay,
A matter much more in my way:
With yon sweet Girl I 'd rather speak
Than him the Academic Greek,
Or wander with this pensive maid,
Than Tully in his classic shade;
One smile from those dear lips, I vow,
Sylvia! would make me happy now!
For I do fear some inward ail,

Thou look'st so deadly still, and pale.
O grief! what can it—can it be?
Is there no end to Misery?

———

Enter SYLVIA, STEPHANIA, ROSELLE, JACINTHA,
and Peasant-girls following.

STEPHANIA. Alas! alas! she is distract—

JACINTHA. Ay, truly: you may know it by her
hands locked so; and her streaming hair; and her
eye fixed upon the ground as if she were choosing her
steps over a bridge not a hair's breadth. Oh, it is a
piteous condition.

ROSELLE. Sweet Sylvia! Gentle maid!—Go not,
we pr'ythee, towards that haunted wood: do not,
we beseech thee!—She looks at me, but speaks not
—O her eyes! her eyes!

Girls. Go not, our queen! our beauteous sovereign!
—We will kneel to thee, if thou wilt stay.

STEPHANIA. 'T is vain!—she heeds us not.

Third Girl. She seemed to love Jacintha, because
she could talk more gentle folk than we: let Jacintha
pray her not to go.

JACINTHA. [*Embracing* SYLVIA.] O gentle
friend! by this entreating and affectionate kiss—

SYLVIA. No comfort! no!—they are ta'en! they
are ta'en!

JACINTHA. I but offend her.

SYLVIA. Is he not dead, answer me that?—Is not
my mother ta'en?—Why trouble ye me thus?—
Forgive, but leave me!—

JACINTHA. Sweetness, even in her moods and
wilfulness.

Girls.   Let us fall down about her on our knees.

SYLVIA.   Prevent me not, I say!—I will proceed !

[*Exit.*

Peasants.   'T will make her fractious : she will go.
Let us follow her to the extent we dare, and persuade
her back if possible.

[*Exeunt after* SYLVIA.

Scene VI.

In murky dungeon round and wide
And coped with clouds from side to side,
Behold a wild, dishevelled form
With eyes like stars in winter storm,
Athwart whose flashing light the rack
Scuds in long wreaths of massy black ;
Behold this form, once noble, and
Even in its mute distraction grand :
Its breast heaves with enormous ire,
Its very nostril teems with fire ;
Its clenched hands are tossing high,
And seem to threat the lowering sky ;
Brain-pierced, heart-stung, and mad as foam,
It paces the infernal dome,
Like an indignant God of Wind
To cloister'd mountain-cave confined.
   In guise so fierce who could discover
Sylvia's once kind and gentle lover ?
But cast your wondering eyes above,
And see within a proud alcove
Two figures seated : this one bears
A crown and sceptre; this appears
A shepherdess : the monarch, he

Toys with her wanton curls, and she
Repays the courtship of her tresses
With amorous looks, and light caresses.
This is the mystic cause, I ween,
Of all our Youth's distracted mien,
The Phantom revelry deceives
His visual sense ; and he believes
Sylvia doth here a recreant prove
To Faith, to Purity, and Love.
    What outward grief, what corporal pain,
Could touch a lover's heart and brain
Like this sharp visionary wo
That wings the tortured fancy so ?
Then, shall we blame the sufferer ?—No !
High though the waves of passion brim,
Pardon we must, and pity him.

———

ROMANZO.   Endure ! O heart ! endure !—
O strings of passion, break not !—Hold but firm
Till I have sealed this iron tomb : burst then,
Fountain of life, and let me choke with blood !—
Thou fair iniquity ! I 'll reach thy locks,
And strangle thee in their twisted goldenness !—
Might, double-thew my limbs ! Knot the great
        sinews,
That my tough, boughy arms curl with their strength,
Like the prodigious elm : I would pull down
To dust these riotous lovers !—Foul abortion !—
I will—O words !—For thee, young treachery !
Beautiful sin ! fair hypocrite ! I 'll paint
Thy cheek a bloodier hue !—O is this earth
Limed to retain me ?—Though my feet do move,
Weights, huge as millstones, seem to clog their steps,
Locking me to this goal—Torture of sight !

What ! wilt thou wind thy passionate arms about
    him ?—
Kiss him not, wanton !
  Phantom of ARARACH.   Fairer than fair !
  Phantom of SYLVIA.   Sweet king !
  ROMANZO.   O scorpion words !—Vile pair !—
    Must I yet storm
Like the fixt oak with idly threatening arms,
Uttering loud tempest-talk, swung with blind rage,
But spur-bound to a spot?
  Phantom of SYLVIA. Look, here's a wreath :
                    [*To the Phantom-king.*
I 'll twist it round thy brow.
  ROMANZO.   Cruel ! oh cruel !
That was my crown ! my garland !
  Phantom of ARARACH.   Come and claim it.
Knock off his miry fetters there !
  Phantom of SYLVIA.   Poor fool !
  ROMANZO. Vengeance ! I 'm free !—Now, you
    luxurious pair,
Have at your hot alcove !—In war, in war
I 've leap'd a battlement Alp-high to this.
  Phantom of ARARACH. Work up ! work up !—
    Dismiel, thou art too slow !
  ROMANZO.   Ha, what is this?—O grief !—the
    dungeon sides
Arise like murky clouds at thunder-call,
Hanging a rocky ciel above my head,
Ready to crush me if I breathe !—
  Phantom of ARARACH.   Let down,
Let down our shafted stairs !—Mount, worshipper
Thine eyes must ache with lowly adoration.
Courage, and knee our throne.
             [*A golden staircase is let down.*

ROMANZO.   Where lead these steps?—
Or how do they come here?—Ah ! Pity stoops
Half out of Heaven, and to her bracelet links
This stair, that I on earth may groan no more,
But creep along her arm into her bosom,
And, like a hurt babe in its mother's breast,
Lament myself to peace !
  Phantom of SYLVIA.   Sir brideman, come !
We can not tarry longer for thy torch
To light us bedward.
  Phantom of ARARACH.   Raise the nuptial song !
Music may draw him, though our love do not.
  ROMANZO.   Am I spell-stricken, now?—Now are
      my feet
Riveted ! bolted ! chained ! that I forbear
To mount to my revenge ?—Hold fast ! hold fast,
Ye silver-clouted stars !—Afford me still
This pendulous step-inviter to your sphere,
I 'll up as swift as soaring Victory
To clap at Heaven-gate her triumphant wings !—
I come ! I come !
          [*As he approaches, the steps fade away.*
Sdeath ! do mine eyes melt at the flaming gold?
  [*Phantoms of* ARARACH *and* SYLVIA.   Ha ! ha !—
      the rainbow-grasper weeps to see
His vision—air !
  ROMANZO.   Justice ! justice, ye gods !
Is this your equity ?—   [*The stair vanishes entirely*
                  I 'll pray no more
The absent Powers.   Justice long since, now Hope,
Ev'n Hope, hath left this planet !—Blank Despair,
Thou only dost abide !—Lend me a sword ;
'T is all I crave, and what thou lov'st to proffer :
A sword, kind deity of the miserable !

Let fall a sword, and I will swear thy name
Sweeter than Mercy's to the wretch in dread
Of everlasting pain !

> [*A sword falls upon the ground.*

Thanks !—Now farewell,
Earth, and its woes for ever !

> [*Phantoms of* ARARACH *and* SYLVIA. Ha ! ha ! ha !

> [*Laughter above.*

ROMANZO.   Nay, let me pause !
There's something dread and horrid in that joy !—
'T is said the fiends laugh where the angels weep :—
I will not do 't !—O all-disposing Heaven,
Pour down thy sorrows as thou wilt, I 'll drink them
In patience, though in tears !

> *Phantoms of* ARARACH *and* SYLVIA.   Ill done !
> O rage !   [*Murmurs above.*

ROMANZO.   Now may I know Heaven smiles upon
>   my deed,   •
For Hell is most unhappy.

> *Phantoms of* ARARACH *and* SYLVIA.   Let's provoke
> him !

> [*The Canopy, with the Phantom-lovers descends.*
> *Phantom of* ARARACH.   Behold !
> *Phantom of* SYLVIA.   Thy rival ! O behold !
> *Phantom of* ARARACH.   Thy love !

ROMANZO.   To death and darkness, with one
>   lightning-sweep
Of this blue thunderbolt !

[*His sword divides the Canopy, which vanishes with
    the Phantoms, displaying the Enchanted Vale and*
    SYLVIA *beside her lover.*

> SYLVIA.   [*Leaping to his bosom.*]   My life ! my
>   lord !—
Take me into thine arms ! take me !—

ROMANZO.   Avaunt !
By what reed nature dost thou only bow
Beneath my stormy hand ? Dares thy slight insolence
Brave me again ?
SYLVIA.   Nay, I will kneel for death,
So my lord wills it !   [*Kneels.*
ROMANZO.   Good ! O art o' the sex !
How well she does it !
SYLVIA.   Come ! I 'll bind mine eyes,
Or cast them on the ground, lest their fond looks
Persuade thee into pity. I would die !
In sooth, I would ! now I have lost thy love.
ROMANZO.   Perfidiousness !—
SYLVIA.   Kill me ! O kill me first !
And name me after !—Let me die believing
I am thy dear one still—the simple thought
Would make me kiss the weapon.   Gentle love !
One agony—one agony!   Kill me not twice,
With sorrow, and the sword !
ROMANZO.   Were I not staunch
As Murder, I would melt at this !—Wilt strive ?
Wilt talk ? Wilt question with me ?
SYLVIA.   I will be dumb—
I 'll cross my patient hands upon my breast,
And wait my death as meek as the poor lily
Whose head falls smiling at her slayer's feet.
Or I will clasp thy knees,—thus—thus ! And if
Tears through my blinding hair will come at all,
'T is for thy misery when I am slain.
Now ! while I kiss thy gentler hand—
ROMANZO.   Thus then, [*Raising his sword.*
Die! die, thou traitress—Now, by heavens, she clings,
Clings to me like a babe !—Whate'er she be,
O God ! how pitiful are woman's tears !

SYLVIA. No !—No !—they are not for myself !—

ROMANZO. Go, wretch !
That seem'st so innocent, but art not,—go !
I cannot murder thee : 't is like infanticide !

SYLVIA. Where shall I go?—wretch as I am !

ROMANZO. I care not !—
Anywhere—anywhere !—so it be from me !
Go to thy paramour ; thy sceptred love ;
Thy demon wooer ; whom my sword dispersed,
But slew not : him thou didst caress but now—

SYLVIA. Him ? him ? the Sorcerer ?

ROMANZO. Ay, thou false one ! ay !
With cheeks as flagrant as the sun's in June,
Smiles broad and liberal as she bestows
Whose blush is wine-engender'd ; with such hands
As smooths the unshorn Satyr when he loves,
Or weave his drunken crowns !—Follow him, go !
He 'll perk thee by his side, I dare be sworn,
On his mock throne ; call thee his florid queen ;
While roars that bring down all the vaulted clouds
To quench the clamor, shall proclaim your title
As wide as Shame can hollo ! After him, go !

SYLVIA. 'T is a most hideous dream !—Would I
had waken'd !

ROMANZO. For me,—O that some violent bolt
would fall,
And make me ashes !—some oak-bending storm
Lap me in its wild skirt, and swirl me down
Precipices footed in the raging waves
Where thunder learns to bellow ; where leviathan
Tosses his foam abroad, and to the sands
Sucks down the shrieking mariner ! plunged there,
Ten thousand fathoms deep amid the billows,
I would find out an ever-stunning grave

Where voice of man could never hail me more !
O my brain seethes with fire !—Death ! death ! O
    death !   [*Exit.*

[SYLVIA *retires, and sits down beside a rock with her
               head leaning against it.*

    SYLVIA.   "Wretch ! "—" False-one ! "—" Preci-
        pices ! "—" Grave ! "—" Death ! death ! "—
What is all this !—O, I am crazed ! I 'm crazed !—
Mother ! — Romanzo ! — help me ! — Fool ! Fool !
    silence !—
Ha ! ha ! ha ! ha !—No ; I 'll not laugh ; I 'll sing.

" I 've taught thee Love's sweet lesson o'er,
    A task that is not learn'd by tears :
Was Sylvia e'er so blest before
    In her wild, solitary years?
        Then what does he deserve, the Youth,
        Who made her con so dear a truth ? "

Why, the key to her happiness, that he may rob
her of it, and begone ; leaving her to live on her
scholarship.   Ah, deceiver !

        " Pearly brow, and golden hair,
          Lips that seem to scent the air ;
          Eyes as bright "—

O yes, indeed !

        " Eyes as bright, and sweet, and blue,
          As violets "—

"Violets!" what next? Pah! I forget—"violets!"—

        " Eyes as bright, and sweet, and blue,
          As violets, weeping tears of dew ! "

I have no better words : but they go pat enough ;
and would be sweet, sweet indeed, could the flower
sigh them over my grave ! — O that it were bed-

time! I am a-weary of this sun; and long to sleep beneath the fresh-green turf, with a sweet-briar at my head to entice the nightingale, and a streamlet at my foot to join in the lullaby.

Lullaby! lullaby! there she sleeps,
  With a wild streamlet to murmur around her:
Lullaby! lullaby! still it keeps ·
  That the pale creature may slumber the sounder!

Lullaby! lullaby! wake no mo!
  Says the sweet nightingale toning above her:
Lullaby! lullaby! life is wo
  When a poor maiden is left by her lover!

At least if all maidens be like me!—and pray Heaven, I die ere night of this thorn in my bosom!

    They told him that his love was dead,
      And slept beneath a willow;
    He turned him on his heel, and said,—
      " She chose a roomy pillow!"

So she wept till the very shroud was moist with her tears? Oh, what a kind shepherd! Would I had such another!—But no! Who thinks of Sylvia?— Not even Sylvia, though she is beside herself! ha! ha! ha!—the first jest I ever made in my life, and, without another, it is a most miserable one!—Indeed, indeed, I am not very happy, though I do sing. Where did I end?

      Enter FLORETTA *behind.*

FLORETTA.   O happy sight! O happy hour!
          I 've found my beauteous lady-flower!
          Arise, arise, and come with me,
          Thou 'rt in the realm of perfidy.

M

SYLVIA.   Ay, that's true; it rhymed to *me*—

> They told him that his love was laid
> Beneath a sullen cypress tree :
> Smiling, quoth he, " The silly Maid,
> They say she died for love of me ! "

There was a swain for you !—ha ! ha ! ha ! ha !

FLORETTA.   Oh, see my tears ! Oh, hear my cries !
> My love ! my beauty ! rise ! arise !
> Sit not, I pray thee, chanting there
> Wild ditties to the ruthless air,
> Like the lost Genius of Despair !
> Two fiends are hither winging fast
> To seize my lovely-one at last.
> Sylvia !—Dost hear me ?—

SYLVIA.   Bird !

FLORETTA.   O come !
> Return to thy forgotten home !
> Hear ye not how the valleys mourn—
> " When will our Shepherdess return ? "
> Return ! return ! the rocks of gray
> And murmuring streams and hollows say !

SYLVIA.   Ay, when I have sung my song, indeed !
—when I have sung my song !

> Was Lubin not a generous swain
> To give his love her heart again ?
> He sent her back the sweet love-token,
> The heart ;—but then, indeed—'t was broken !

What does your fairy-hood say to that ?—Do your little goodies spin thread fine and strong enough to bind up a broken heart ?—If so I will buy it of them for a silver penny cut out of the moon.   Bear them my offer : I will sing here till you come back.

FLORETTA.

Ah, stay not ! stay not ! lily mine !
Come o'er, come o'er the demon line !
One moment, and the line is crost !
One moment, and my flower is lost !—
Wilt thou not listen to my wo ?
Would I neglect my Sylvia so ?
Once when I was thy favourite ouphe
Thou could'st not pet me half enough ;
But now to any nook I may,
And weep myself to dew away !—
Ah ! thou wilt come !—in faith thou must !—
I 'll strew thy path with petal-dust,
And brush thy soft cheek with my wing,
As round thee merrily I sing
A gay, light-tripping, frolic song,
To lure thy charmèd steps along.

My Lady sweet ! O come with me
To where the springs of nectar flow,
  And like a cunning cuckoo-bee*
Before thee, I will singing go,
    With *cheer ! cheer ! cheer !*
    When flowery beds or banks appear.

---

* The Moroe, *Cuculus Indicator*, Cuckoo-bee, or Honey-guide, is a little bird of the African deserts, gifted with a most peculiar tact for discovering the nests of wild bees, and a still more remarkable one for participating in their contents. When it has gotten the wind of such a treasure, it allures by a perpetual cry resembling the words *cheer ! cheer !* any traveller or honey-loving animal it can meet towards the nest ; sits trembling with avidity in a neigbbouring bush, while its companion sacks the magazine ; and finally obtains as a remuneration for its services the relics of the booty.—*Vide Linnæus, Sparrman.*

I 'll lead thee where the festal bees
   Quaff their wild stores of crusted wine,
From censers sweet, and chalices
   With lips almost as red as thine.
     And *cheer ! cheer ! cheer !*
     I 'll cry when such a feast is near.
Sylvia ! O hapless maiden ! Come !

To fairer scenes and brighter bowers
   Than bloom in all the world beside,
Where thou shalt pass Elysian hours,—
   I 'll be thy duteous Honey-guide.
     And *cheer ! cheer ! cheer !*
     Shall be my note through all the year.
Terror ! O terror ! hither they
Bend them with all the might they may
To bear my shepherdess away.
The demons !—Oh, unhappy one !
Art thou enchanted to a stone ?
Up ! up ! or thou art all undone !

     Oh, come ! Oh, come my lady-dove !
     My peerless flower ! my Queen of May !

     Enter GRUMIEL *and* MOMIEL.

   I 'll call thee every name of love,
     If thou wilt wend with me away !
        But wo ! wo ! wo !
        She will not answer ay or no !

GRUMIEL.   Ha ! ha ! have we caught thee at last ?
MOMIEL.   Napping, i' faith ! like a wildcat, with
her eyes open. Come ! bring her along.
FLORETTA.   O my lost flower ! my flower !
MOMIEL.   Ay, *Trip-Madam* is her name: see
how kindly she comes to it !

GRUMIEL. What is that hizzing thing there?

MOMIEL. Why, nothing less than three barley-corns' length of woman-kind, in a huge petticoat made of a white thumbstall, and having wings as long as a brown hornet's or a caterpillar's after conversion. A pocket-piece!—She, too, has a name. *Busybody*. Wilt come with us, Gad-about?

GRUMIEL. No! we have more of the sex by one than is welcome.

MOMIEL. Nay, thou may'st flutter and squeal and ricket about, like an old wren (as thou art!) when the schoolboy filches thy young one. Adieu, mistress! and bear my respects to *Monsieur* Saint Vitus, thy dancing-master.

GRUMIEL. Come on, thou gibbering ape!

MOMIEL. Then, I may say, like one of my kindred in the fable, putting my hand upon this wig-block of thine,— "Bless me! what a fine head were this, if it only had brains!"

GRUMIEL. I'll—

MOMIEL. Go! go on!—Take a graybeard's advice : never open thy mouth but to eat thy porridge. Though thou didst live upon garbage, nothing would ever go into thy throat that was not better than aught that came out of it. Go on, pray thee!—Despise not the use of thy trotters,—Good-bye, little Mistress Hop o' my thumb!—warm work for an afternoon, Mistress! Thou look'st for all the world like a humming-top on the wing; and indeed wouldst make a most lively representation of the proverb—a reel in a bottle. Go on, buzzard!

[*Exeunt Fiends with* SYLVIA.

FLORETTA. Now may I to some covert creep,
          And like the secret bird of sorrow

In darkling tears for ever weep,
Nor bid again the sun good morrow !
And *wo ! wo ! wo !*
Shall be my note where'er I go.
                              [*Vanishes.*

Scene VII.

The fairy camp, with tents displayed,
Squadrons and glittering files arrayed
In strict battalia o'er the plain :
Gay trumpets sound the shrill refrain ;
From field to field loud orders ring,
And couriers scour from wing to wing.
On a soft ambling jennet-fly
And girt with elfin chivalry
Who mingle in suppressed debate,
Rides forth the pigmy Autocrat.
Her ivory spear swings in its rest,
Close and succinct her martial vest
Tucked up above her snowy knee,
A miniature Penthesilee !
Her Amazonian nymphs beside
Their queen, at humble distance ride ;
Encased in golden helms their hair,
In corslets steel their bosoms fair,
With trowsered skirt loopt strait and high
Upon the limb's white luxury,
That clasps so firm, yet soft, each steed
Thinks himself manfully bestrid,
And snorts and paws with fierce delight,
Proud of his own young Maiden-knight,

Whose moony targe at saddle-bow
Hangs loose, and glimmers as they go.
   Now breathe your fifes and roll your drums,
'T is the Queen's Majesty that comes !

MORGANA.   Look out !—look out ! — Floretta
    should be here ;
Or Osme whom we sent.   [*Exeunt scouts.*
                 Nephon, droop not,
Thou didst perform thy careful duty well !
Rash and presumptuous youth ! he merits all
The punishment he suffers : To neglect
The warning that thou gav'st him ere he past
Insolent o'er the bounds, where his perdition
Gaped for him, like the monster of the Nile,
In every brake and jungle !
   NEPHON.   Madam, indeed,
I told him 't was a fiendish stratagem,
To lure him over, but he would not hear ;
Stampt when I pluckt his skirt, and swung his sword
Round by the wrist, so that I 'd lost my hold
And hand together, but I let him go.
   MORGANA. I know, I saw it ; thou art not to
    blame,
Proud of his azure weapon, he would cope
With those who scorn it, as they do the edge
Of bladed feather, or those grassy swords
Which our soft tourneyers wield—
   [*Cry without.*]   A messenger !

Enter OSME.

   MORGANA. Where is thy sister ? hast thou seen
    her, say ?

OSME.   Here comes the elve, weeping her silent
way :
Some dreadful news I wot she brings
So lost in grief the wretch appears,
Her head she hides between her wings,
And cannot tell her tale for tears !

MORGANA.   The Maid is lost !—Arm ! arm, ye
warlike elves !
With potent virtues now endue yourselves ;
Lay by your puppet words and spears and shields,
We must prepare for other fights and fields.
Mount ! mount with me in clouds the blackening
sky !
War be the word, and Battle be the cry !

———————

Scene VIII.

O thou dread Bard ! whose soul of fire
Moved o'er the dark-string'd Epic lyre
Till brightening where thy spirit swept
Lustre upon its dimness crept,
And at thy word, from dull repose
The Light of heavenly Song arose !
O that this lyric shell of mine
Were like thy harp, Minstrel divine !
With thunder-chords intensely strung,
To chime with thy audacious song
That scorned all deeds to chronicle
Less than the wars of Heaven and Hell :
O that this most despised hand
Could sweep so beautifully grand
The nerves Tyrtæan !—I would then

Storm at the souls of little men,
And raise them to a nobler mood
Than that Athenian master could ! *
But no !—the spirit long has fled
That warmed the old tremendous dead,
Who seem in stature of their mind
The Anaks of the human kind :
So bright their crowns of glory burn,
Our eyes are seared ; we feebly turn
In terrible delight away,
And only—" Ye were mighty !" say.
We turn to forms of milder clay,
Who smile indeed, but cannot frown,
Nor bring Hell up nor Heaven down.
One gloomy Thing indeed, who now
Lays in the dust his lordly brow,
Had might, a deep indignant sense,
Proud thoughts, and moving eloquence ;
But oh ! that high poetic strain
Which makes the heart shriek out again
With pleasure half mistook for pain ;
That clayless spirit which doth soar
To some far empyrean shore,
Beyond the chartered flight of mind,
Reckless, repressless, unconfined,
Spurning from off the roofed sky
Into unciel'd Infinity ;
Beyond the blue crystalline sphere
Beyond the ken of optic seer,
The flaming walls of this great world,
Where Chaos keeps his flag unfurled

---

* Tyrtæus, the Attic pedagogue, before the sound of whose
lyre the walls of Ithome fell.

And embryon shapes around it swarm,
Waiting till some all-mighty arm
Their different essences enrol
Into one sympathetic whole ;
That spirit which presumes to seize
On new creation-seeds like these,
And bears on its exultant wings
Back to the earth undreamt-of things,
Which unseen we could not conceive,
And seen we scarcely can believe ;—
That strain, this spirit, was not thine,
Last favour'd child of the fond Nine !
Great as thou wert, thou lov'dst the clod,
Nor like blind MILTON walked with God !
Him who dared lay his hand upon
The very footstool of Jove's throne,
And lift his intellectual eye
Full on the blaze of Deity :
Who sang with the celestial choir
Hosanna ! to the Eternal Sire ;
And trod the holy garden, where
No man but he and Adam were ;
Who reach'd that high Parnassian clime
Where Homer sat as gray as Time,
Murmuring his rhapsodies sublime !
Who from the Mantuan's bleeding crown
Tore the presumptuous laurel down,
And fix'd it, proudly, on his own !
Who with that Bard diviner still
Than Earth has seen or ever will,
The pride, the glory of the hill,
Albion ! thy other deathless son,—
Reigns ; and with them the Grecian one,
Leagued in supreme tri-union !

Then why should I, whose dying song
Shall ne'er be wept thy reeds among,
Lydian Cayster !—I, no bird
Of that majestic race which herd
Upon thy smoothly-rolling surge,
And sing their own departing dirge ;
But one who must, O bitter doom !
Sink mutely to my sullen tomb
Amid this lone deserted stream,
Whose sands shall pillow my death-dream,
And for my hollow knell shall teem
Its dittying waters over me !
Why should I so adventurous be
With imitative voice to pour
One strain Cayster heard before ?

To stretch that bow should I pretend,
Which none but thou, dread Bard ! could bend,
Well might the uncheck'd thunder speed,
Full volley, to avenge the deed,
And blast me, impious : but I keep
Dread finger still upon my lip,
And inly to Suggestion say—
"Lead not that high heroic way ;
Where Milton trod few mortals may !"—
The war of Fiends and Virtuous Powers,
Sing thou in thy celestial bowers,
And charm the bright seraphic throng
Who crowd to hear the rapturous song,
And at their old recorded fame
Glow doubly bright. Not mine the same
High audience, nor a theme so high,
Nor oh ! such passing minstrelsy !

Wise in my weakness, I forego
The deeds of fell contest to show,

When Demon power met Godly host,
And battlefield was won and lost.
This has been sung in higher strain
Than ever shall be heard again !
I only tell ye to behold
A scene in sulphury volumes rolled
And hear within the clang of arms,
With shouts and dissonant alarms :
There came a mighty crash !—a pause
As dread succeeds—O righteous cause !
Be thine that note of victory
Which shakes the pillars of the sky
With loud symphonious melody !

————

CHORUS *of Spirits within.*
Victory !—
Victory !—Lo ! the fight is done !
Victory !—Lo ! the field is won !
Victory ! O victory !
Rejoice, ye glorious harps ! rejoice !
Proclaim with one harmonious voice
Victory ! Victory ! Victory !

[*Enter the Fairy Host in triumph.*]
Victory !—
Victory !—Lo ! the fiends are fled !
Victory !—Lo ! their king is dead !
Victory ! O victory !
Pronounce it with your silver tones
And shining mouths, sweet clarions !
Victory ! Victory ! Victory.

Victory !—
Victory !—Lo ! the welkin clears !
Victory !—Lo ! the sun appears !
Victory ! O Victory

The Powers of Darkness yield the glen,
So breathe sweet harp and trump again—
  Victory ! Victory ! Victory !
     [Exeunt rejoicing.

Scene IX.

The smoothest greensward, dry and shorn,
Where glowing sundrops seem to burn
Like ardent tears from Phœbus' eye
Fallen in golden showers from high.
Primroses, king-cups, cuckoo-buds,
And pansies cloakt in yellow hoods,
And splendid, bosom-button'd daisies
With grandam ruffs, and saucy faces :
The moss is hoar with very heat
And crisp as frost-work to the feet.
Oh, such a place to dance a round
To the hot timbrel's dingling sound !
And when the booming finger runs
Around its orb,—to hear the tones
Of shrill pipe speaking in between,
Like high-voiced woman 'mid hoarse men,
Tossing the head from side to side
To suit the humorous tune applied,
And stamping with uneasy glee
Till the wild reel has come to thee.
Then how the buxom lass is swung,
Scarce knowing why or where she 's flung ?
The kerchief dropt, and bosom glowing
Over its silken border flowing,
And the trim kirtle whirling high
Shows the wrought garter's rainbow tie.

But oh ?—oh, whither do I stray
From sense and scope so far away !
Thou syren Girl, with flowing hair,
Hymné ! how sweet thy pleasures are !
Let me but hear thy trancing lyre
Sing " Come away ! "—no foot of fire,
Burning with messages to Jove,
Transcends my haste to her I love.
Thee, thee I follow, half unseen,
Through endless vales and forests green,
O'er wilds and browy mountains stern,
Lone heaths and pastures red with fern,
From rock to cave, from lake to stream,
Fast fleeting like a noiseless stream
Where'er I see thy beauty beam :
Ev'n though thy most seductive smile
Leads me erroneous all the while !
As the bee mourning tracks the flower
That winds bear offward from its bower,
So, murmuring all my way, I roam
To find thy sweetness in some home,
Some verdurous nook, where tiptoe I
Put back the froward greenery,
To hear the attraction of thy tongue
Bowing the woods to drink its song.
Oh ! well for me thou art not one
Living in the green deeps alone,
Or banding with the Sisters three,
Who drown men with their melody :
For did'st thou call me through the roar
Of wild waves on a cliffy shore,
Where billowy Ocean's lion trains
Shake into surge their hoary manes,
My knell should that same day be rung
Blind Nereus' chapell'd caves among.

Then leave, ah ! leave me to my story !
Begone thou with thy crown of glory !
Unless thou drop one wreath on me,
What should I care, slight Nymph ! for thee ?

STEPHANIA, ROSELLE, JACINTHA, ANDREA, GERONYMO, *and Peasants, assembled. They perform a dance;* ANDREA, *between* STEPHANIA *and* ROSELLE *as partners.*

STEPHANIA.   Nay, I can foot it no longer.

ROSELLE.   Nor I, in faith ! I cannot feel my legs under me.   Signior Andrea, you must dance to that oaken stump, if you will not sit down with the rest of us.   O my heart bounces so, it will break my girdle !

JACINTHA.   Well, all is happy now.   Our beautiful Queen and her partner are restored.

Second Peasant.   Ay, and here is an entertainment the hospitable dame has provided to welcome us all. Would the hostess were now at the head of her table !

Third Peasant.   Ay, would she were !—Jollity has set in for the evening.

ROSELLE.   If it would only last till doomsday, we might be satisfied !

GERONYMO.   We are, we are satisfied !   We are all blessed ones, that is the tot of the matter !

STEPHANIA.   And our unlucky friend there is the happiest of us all.   He has not yet finished his setting-step to his stumpy partner.

First Girl.   Lawk ! what a skip-jack ! what a bounce-about !—How he cuts !

Second Girl. How he capers! He must have been a rope-dancer, as sure as sure——

Fourth Peasant. Was he ever on the stage, think ye?

GERONYMO. Absolutely he was, absolutely: I saw him myself there; namelessly, or, that is to say, on the top of a barrel.

Third Girl. Is this he I have heard of under the name of Merry Andrew?

ROSELLE. No wonder if it was, for he is the merriest rogue—Oh! I do love that impudent smock-face of his!

JACINTHA. I thinks he looks as if he were about to jump out of his skin with joy.

STEPHANIA. All his afflictions are at an end. He has not even a bone in his foot to complain of.

ANDREA [*stopping short*]. Oh, misery of miseries! Oh, unspeakable misfortune!

ROSELLE. Mercy upon us! what new calamity?

ANDREA. Oh, that a man cannot have two wives at a time!—I could find it in my heart to turn Turk for the privilege.

ROSELLE. Ho! ho! Signior Doleful!—is it this that afflicts you?

STEPHANIA. I thought there was another face under that hood.

ANDREA. What say you, Cherry bud? would you have me?—And you, Sweet lips?

STEPHANIA. By your leave, signior: either or neither.

ROSELLE. Come, tell us honestly now: what kind of a husband should you make? How should you behave were you married to either of us simple maidens!

ANDREA. Hang myself incontinently.'

STEPHANIA. O pretty !—hang yourself if married to either !

ANDREA. Ay ; in despair for the other. But if I were only married to both — ye Graces! what a trio we should make I what a picture for a painter ! —Would there be anything, do you think, on this side of the sky to compare with us ?

ROSELLE. No, certainly ; unless it were a white goose between a couple of grey ones.

ANDREA. Holla !

STEPHANIA. Or an ass between two thistles.

ANDREA. O gemini !

ROSELLE. Or the likeness would be more like if we said, a crab-apple between two cherries.

STEPHANIA. Or, as it is in the church, a figure of Death between two angels.

ANDREA. Astonishment !—I profess the women have tongues !—Tongues apiece, as I live, to do evil.

STEPHANIA. Ay, and more than that—

ANDREA. What I more than one tongue apiece ? —O monstrous !

STEPHANIA. No, signior ; but we have the use of that we possess, as you shall find if you please to set it a-going.

ANDREA. By that bunch of keys at your girdle I know you to be a housekeeper, and therefore a person worthy of credit ; I will take your word in this matter. — [*To* GERONYMO.] Well, friend !— What a bowing dost thou keep there ? as if thou wast upper man of a saw pit !—Is this what you call scraping an acquaintance?

GERONYMO. [*To* STEPHANIA.] O imperious

N

mistress of my heart !—Suffering-queen of my affections !—I cannot say what I could say, nor will I speak what I would speak !

ANDREA.   Write it then, write it !   If your tongue is bound to keep the peace on this ground, take her on some other.   Inscribe her a billet-doux, and let it be as full of compliments as if it were her epitaph ; let it breathe professions like the air of a minister's levee-room ; stick it all over with sweet words, as a pastry cook does a tart with comfits ; and, in the end, let me advise you, as one that knows the fashion, to subscribe it — "yrs. faithfully ; " yours faithfully, which is as much as to say—Put your whole trust in me, and fear not !

GERONYMO.   I will ! I will do so !   And I will take care, as you say, not to admit — " yours faithfully ! " it has a most porpoise-like air with it !

STEPHANIA.   O Geronymo ! you need not be porpoise-like to gain me : you are already a melting creature !

ANDREA.   Pooh ! have we been conjuring up a whirlwind to blow gossamer !   This is a quail, indeed ! that comes, fat and foolish, at the first pipe of the sportsman.   Well ! the vanities of this life are enough to make any man a crying philosopher. — Hark ye, ladies ! [*To* JACINTHA *and* ROSELLE.] What say you to a glee, or catch, or chorus ?—Li ! ti ! lirra ! tirra !—Eh, temptresses ? eh, you pair of wild pigeons ?

JACINTHA.   Roselle chants like a green linnet ; but I—

ANDREA.   No, you cannot sing at all : I 'd swear it, from the shape of your neck.   It is made like an

ivory pipe, only to be played upon with the fingers ;
and a man must put his lips to your mouth if he would
produce sweet music. Come, I 'll charm it out of you.

JACINTHA.   Not so free, brother.

ROSELLE.   Not quite so free, Signior Rolypolillo !

ANDREA.   Bless me ! have I got into a mountain-
nunnery ?—Well ; it is all one to me ; I have my
kisses, and you have your lips. If you will not
embrace your good fortune when it offers, 't is your
own loss. I know there will be biting of nails for it
in private : but never come with your tilly-vally to
me ! never presume even to blow me a favour ! I had
rather kiss, ay, a thousand times, the brim of this
delicious goblet, than the lips of the Empress of
Morocco herself, though they say her mouth might
be taken for a bee hive.   [*Drinks.*

Second Peasant.   He should have gills like a fish,
to let all he gulps pass out behind his ears.

ANDREA.   Come, lasses, a glee ! a glee ! My pipe
is as mellow as a French horn. Come ; you have
nothing to do but say *hem ! hem !*—put your right
hand under your left breast to show that your heart
is beating—and then, with an interesting droop of the
head, thus, as if you offered your neck to a scimitar,
and, indeed, la ! had much rather die than exhibit
your faculty,—begin *expressivo e amabile,* raising your
voice by degrees till it bullies the echo, and almost
breaks your sweet heart-strings as short as maccaroni.
Allons !   "Tirra lee !"

> Two sweet Maidens sang together
>   Tirra lirra ! tirra lee !
> Comes a Swain, and asks them whether
>   He might join their tirra lee !
>   O how happy, happy he,
>   Might he join their tirra lee

To his prayer the nymphs replying—
Tirra lirra ! tirra lee !
Kept the silly shepherd sighing
Still to join their tirra lee !
O how happy, &c.

Nought they said unto his suing,
Nought but—tirra lirra lee !
For they loved to keep him wooing,
Still to join their tirra lee !
O how happy, &c.

Looking sad while they were laughing,
What the silly clown ! does he ?
Takes, in mere despair, to quaffing
Sweeter far than tirra lee !   [*Drinks.*

ROSELLE.   A good excuse !
JACINTHA.   His modesty had some need of it.
ANDREA.   O how happy, happy he
Pouring out his tirra lee !

Enter AGATHA, SYLVIA, *and* ROMANZO.

As I live, madam, your wine-merchant is an honest
fellow : this is excellent champagne as ever I
drank at five-and-sixpence a bottle !—though, indeed,
a little too potent of the gooseberry.

Peasants.   All joy attend our Queen ! our Queen !
the lady of our hearts !—our sovereign princess !—the
star of our worships !—the idol of our perfections !—
Huzza ! our May-Queen ! our May-Queen !

SYLVIA.   Thanks, kind friends and neighbours !
Would I were indeed a queen for some few hours,
that I might reward, by other means than these ac-
knowledgments, your love and loyalty !   But though
my coffers are empty, my heart is full, and you shall
partake largely of its affections.   Welcome to you all !

AGATHA. Welcome ! welcome, friends and neighbours !

Peasants. Does she not speak very queen-like ?— so courtsying, and gracious, and withal so high-spoken and indignified !—Oh, if our duke had only seen her before he married the proud French princess, with her nose turned up like the toe of a Chinaman's slipper !—Well ! to see the luck of foreigners in this country ! we make hothouse plants of them, and leave our own pretty flowers to the will of the weather !

ROMANZO. [*to* ANDREA] I may freely pardon you for what you did unwittingly : but let me beseech you for the future to keep a stricter guard upon your tongue, whose volubility is ever laying you open to your enemies.

ANDREA. Here she is, sir, in petticoat regimentals (*Pointing at Roselle*) : this is she who will stand sentinel over my volatility ; this is my body-guard, my life-guard, my beef-eater, who will never let me travel the length of her apron string without keeping, I dare swear for her, watch and ward upon my actions. What other guard would you have me set over my tongue, unless I were to go muzzled like a terrier in the dog-days?

ROSELLE. Never doubt me ! I will stop your mouth—

ANDREA. With kisses : O you are a sad wanton ! —She will always hang upon me thus, sir, as if I wore her for a Spanish cloak, and our lips are always touching like a double-cherry. In a word, sir, she is, poor girl ! so incorrigibly fond of me, that I believe I must, perforce—take her to wife, lest there might be, as they say in England, a suspension of her *habeas corpus*, or some other dreadful calamity, too tedious to mention.

ROSELLE.   I will promise to hang myself for love, when you drown yourself for melancholy.

ROMANZO.   There is surely something very catching in this place.   I should as soon think of your taking a lock-jaw as a love-fever.

ANDREA.   Reform, sir ! reform !—it is the order of the day, and shall be radical in my constitution. I have determined to remedy all abuses, redress all grievances, root out all old prejudices, customs, and inveterate habits, which have so long made a borough of my body ; and to regulate myself in future by a new code, which in a short time I hope and trust will render me—the envy of all my surrounding neighbours, and the admiration of the world !

ROMANZO.   Marriage is the serious end of all our follies.

ANDREA.   Alas ! ay, sir ! It is what we must all come to !   Death and matrimony are both grave words ; and the chief distinction between them is that the halter very often brings us to death, while matrimony very often brings us to the halter.

ROSELLE.   No fear of that with you : if you are to be choked, it will be with a flagon of Rhenish.

ANDREA.   But the upshot of the whole is, there is nothing left me now but—conjugal felicity.   I have been, it is true, while in your worship's company, little better than a reprobate ; now that I have kept this lady's, I am little better than one of the converted.   In a word, sir, this nymph has made a prototype of me, and I only await your benediction. From having been, as you know, sir, a perfect she-Timon, or in other words, a manhater of all womankind, I am now, in all love-matters, become as faithful and fond as a green turtle !--Come, sir, pray give away the bridegroom : I shall never have courage to throw myself into her arms without your paternal countenance.

STEPHANIA.   O the Virgin ! how he blushes !

ROSELLE.   In good truth, sweetheart, if bashfulness had been the only stumbling-block in the way of your promotion, you would never have broken your shins over it.   However, I like you better than if you were ever so modest.

ROMANZO.   Well then, come, I will bestow your innocence upon this maiden—

GERONYMO.   So please your reverence, and mine too upon Mistress Stephania.   She will be much beholden to your reverence for the donation.

ANDREA.   Ha ! ha ! ha ! ha ! your worship is like to have all the modesty of the country at your disposal, if you will take it under your protection.

ROMANZO.   Truly I have no desire to meddle with it : you and honest Geronymo must endeavour to get rid of the troublesome commodity without my assistance.   I dare say you will experience no impediment from your partners.

ANDREA.   'Pon my feracity ! I apprehend there will be no let in that quarter : eh, brother Sheepface ?

GERONYMO.   You have said it, you have said it : there 't is, and that is the tot of the matter !

ROMANZO.   Our hostesses are seated.

AGATHA.   You are so full of joy, that you seem to want no other nourishment.

Peasants.   Should not our Queen sit under the Maybush at the head of the table ?

ROMANZO.   True, neighbours, it should be so. Come, fairest ! you shall take your state, and I will be your cupbearer.

Sylvia. No, you must sit beside me, else I shall be like many a real queen, unhappy in my splendour. If I be indeed queen, you must obey me in this. Come, sit, sit. Sit, fair companions, and let each shepherd choose his place next the lass who will make room for him. But hearken !—Ere we touch what is set before us, it is meet that we return solemn thanks for our happy deliverance from peril and sorrow to that Power which has befriended us in our extremity.

FINAL CHORUS.

Sweet Bards have told
That Mercy droppeth as the gentle rain
From the benignant skies ;
And that in simple-hearted times of old,
Praise unto Heaven again
Did in a fragrant cloud of incense rise !

Thus the great sun
Breathes his wide blessing over herb and flower,
Which bloom as he doth burn ;
And to his staid yet ever-moving throne,
They from the mead and bower
Offer a grateful perfume in return.

So then should we,
Whom Pity hath beheld with melting eye,
Utter our hymns of praise,
In solemn joy and meek triumphancy
Unto the Powers on high :
Raise then the song of glory ! Shepherds raise !

THE END.

TURNBULL AND SPEARS, PRINTERS, EDINBURGH.